SINNER'S POSSESSION

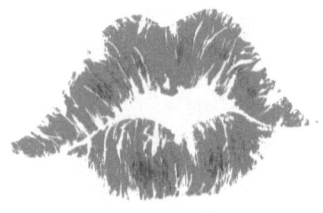

EVERNIGHT PUBLISHING ®

www.evernightpublishing.com

SAM CRESCENT

Copyright© 2021

Sam Crescent

Editor: Karyn White

Cover Art: Sour Cherry Designs

Jacket Design: Jay Aheer

ISBN: 978-0-3695-0311-4

SINNER'S POSSESSION

SINNER'S POSSESSION

Chaos Bleeds, 9

Sam Crescent

Copyright © 2017

Chapter One

"Why do you look fucking miserable?" Butler asked.

Sinner dropped into a seat at the Chaos Bleeds clubhouse bar. He wasn't in the best of moods, and hearing that question from Butler just made him even angrier. He wanted to hit someone or hurt someone, anything to get rid of this frustrated feeling that was consuming him. He fucking hated it, and wanted it gone.

All of his life he had gone after whatever he wanted, and consequences be damned. Being with Chaos Bleeds had always been his one constant, until Lola came along. She had become part of his world, and now, he was going to lose her, he felt it.

"Shut the fuck up, and pour me a drink," he said, looking at the large bottles of beer behind Butler. "Doesn't this shit hurt you?" He pointed at all the alcohol. Butler had been one of the biggest addicts in the club. He'd been clean and sober for many years now.

"Nope, not anymore. I can serve drinks, smell the stuff, and it doesn't cause me a problem at all. I'm happily drinking my very nice, fruity iced tea," Butler said. To emphasize his point, he grabbed a large tall glass filled with a red flavored tea. "Yum."

When they had been back in Fort Wills, Angel had made the concoction one summer. Butler had been complaining about the complete lack of fresh drinks. Within twenty minutes, Angel was there, drink in hand, and Butler was her slave for life.

Butler handed him a bottle of beer. "Drink up, and tell me your problems."

"I don't have any."

"Please. It's a Friday afternoon, and you're here like a junkie getting his fix. Something is up, and you can pretend all you want. I'm not buying it, babe."

Sinner sighed, running fingers through his hair, which had grown out in the past few months. He pulled out a letter and handed it over to Butler.

"You're stealing Lola's mail now? I think this has stalker written all over it."

He rolled his eyes. "Read it."

Butler sighed, looking uncomfortable. "Reading women's mail is almost as bad as going through their underwear drawer."

"Just read it, please. I want to know that I'm not going out of my mind."

"Dude, I could have told you that years ago. You're out of your mind." Butler went to hand the letter back.

"I need help, and you know I hate asking."

"You're right. You hate asking for anything. Fine, fine, fine." Butler pulled the letter out and began to read.

Sinner tapped his fingers on the top of the counter, waiting.

After seconds, maybe even minutes passed, Sinner had enough. "Well, what do you think?"

Butler folded it back up and placed it inside the envelope. "Lola has been offered an apprenticeship at a technology firm. Why does this come as a shock for you?"

"She didn't tell me about it, and there is a date on the calendar today."

"Wait, she's going to go for the job?" Butler asked.

"I don't know. Over the past few months, she's been pulling away from me. I really don't know her anymore, or any of the shit that is going on inside her head. The nightmares are back as well."

Lola had been taken from the street, repeatedly raped and beaten by the enemy of The Skulls and Chaos Bleeds. He'd been known as "Master", but he had in fact been a brother to Gash, a member of the Skulls. Anyway, they had found her, brought her home, protected her, and he'd fallen in love with her. He'd changed his womanizing ways for her, and she was still pulling away from him. He didn't like it.

She was the first woman in the world to make him care. Rubbing at the pain in his chest, he took a long swallow of his beer.

"Do you even know if she's gone to this? She's big friends with Angel and Lacey. Maybe she went to Fort Wills. She is always heading there to see her friends."

"Tell me, Butler, a woman like Lola, would she pass this up?" Sinner asked.

Butler sighed, looking at the piece of paper. "A

woman with Lola's experience, then I say no. A woman that has had her talent used against her, caused her to have those nightmares, then no, she wouldn't. We make her feel safe. She has a family here because she has denied her other family. I think you need to talk to Lola about this."

"What are you losers talking about?" Simon asked, climbing up onto a barstool, and resting his arms. For an eight-year-old kid, he was growing fast. He lifted one finger. "Give me a beer, buddy, if you know what is good for you."

Simon was Devil's first son, and even that came with its own drama. For instance, Lexie wasn't his mother. Lexie's dead sister was Simon's mother. They were all sworn to secrecy about that.

"Hey, kid. We're having woman issues," Sinner said, leaning in. They all loved this little guy. He was quirky and so funny.

"Problem with the ladies, I get it," Simon said. "I'm the man."

Butler burst out laughing. "Here you go, tough guy." He placed an orange soda in front of Simon.

"Cheers. There's only one girl I love."

Butler and Sinner looked at each other, and said the one name they heard all the time.

"Tabby!"

Even Simon spoke, and they all laughed. Tabby was Tiny's little girl, Tiny who had once been Prez of The Skulls.

Yeah, that was future drama.

Sinner took a large swig of his beer.

"I heard Mom talking, and she said that if you squeeze a bar of soap too tightly, it slips out," Simon said. He showed them what he meant by pressing his hands together, and then imitating the action of the soap spilling out.

"Okay," Sinner said.

"She said that was what you were doing with Lola. That you're squeezing her so tightly that she can't breathe." Simon pretended to choke. "I did that once to Tabitha. She kicked me between the legs. Did Lola kick you?"

Butler chuckled. "Man, you are a hoot. I can't wait until you get older. You're going to drive Devil insane."

Speaking of Devil, the man himself turned up with Laurell in his arms. "Simon, why do I feel you're up to no good?"

"I'm drinking a beer, and hanging with the guys, Dad. You tell me to do that all the time."

"No, I ask you to find some friends for yourself. Your mother is in the kitchen, and she needs you."

Simon fist pumped. "She's going to teach me how to make Tabby's favorite, chocolate pie."

Before Devil could say anything, Simon ran off, and Devil took his seat. "That kid is going to be a nightmare when he's older."

"I think you've got to be more worried about him being a chef for his precious girl."

Devil rolled his eyes, and Sinner felt better about his own problems. "Just out of curiosity, if Simon and Tabitha get together, would our two clubs merge?" Sinner asked.

"Oh, oh, oh, we could be called Chaos Skulls," Butler said.

"Or Skulls Bleeds!"

They started laughing, and Devil shrugged. "If that's what needs to happen, then it happens."

"You're not worried?" Sinner asked, wiping away his tears of laughter.

"Nope."

"What about war between the two clubs?"

"First, Lash wouldn't do that. He'll see the benefit of our two clubs together. Now, Tiny, he's another problem. He'll probably hunt down my son and shoot his ass."

Sinner stared at his Prez. He had a great respect and love for Devil. The man had seen the entire club through thick and thin. No matter what happened, they could all rely on Devil to see the club right.

"You'll let that happen?"

"Of course, I won't let that happen. There's no way I'm letting Tiny hurt my son, but I won't interfere. Simon's young. I've got plenty of time to teach him how to handle himself." Devil cooed to his baby girl.

"You've changed your mind," Butler said.

"I'd say that Lexie has changed my mind. There's no point in fighting with my woman. She knows what is best. Simon and Tabitha, they have this thing. Now, it could fizzle out, or it will go stronger. Either way, I'm not going to push my son."

Sinner agreed. *Kind of like what you're doing with Lola.*

He was protecting his woman. That was all he was doing. He was protecting his woman, loving her, caring for her, and making sure nothing ever hurt her. She'd been hurt enough, and he was tired of the pain she had been through.

"So, Granddad Devil, I think it has a nice ring to it," Butler said.

"I'm too young to be a granddad."

"You do know that Simon will make you one soon, though, right?"

"Not until he's thirty," Devil said.

Sinner looked at Devil, curiosity getting the better

of him. "Okay, I have to ask. How can you guarantee that Simon won't make you a granddad? If he's anything like you, I'd expect sooner than later."

"Unlike you guys, I've got a deal with a doctor. He has promised that when the time is right, he will have a nice long sit down with Simon, about the dangers of not bagging your shit up."

There was silence for several seconds, and then Sinner bent down laughing. "You really think scaring him with STDs and STIs will help. This is just too fucking funny."

Even Butler was laughing his ass off.

Devil stood. "We'll see who is laughing in the end."

"Fifty bucks that Simon makes him a granddad at eighteen?" Butler said.

"No need to make that bet. It's a guarantee."

****

Lola Sparks sat in the café and was thankful that she had only watched the door for ten of the fifteen minutes that she had been sitting there. Her jeans were digging into her stomach. They were a size sixteen, but she had put weight on in the past few months, and she just knew it would only be a matter of time before she was in a size eighteen. Not that her figure bothered Sinner. No, he seemed to love her curves, when he wasn't worrying about everything else. She was in Fort Wills, and it was late, but that was fine for her. This was her excuse for leaving without saying a word.

Her heart was racing as she sat alone. No one approached her, which she was thankful for. She ran her fingers through her black hair that Lacey had dyed for her a couple of weeks ago. She loved coming to this town, even though it did hold a lot of bad memories for her. Shutting down those memories, she lifted her coffee and took a sip.

The Skulls was like a second home to her, and she found herself here more often than not. She adored Angel, the wife of the club's Prez, Lash. Of course, Lola loved the outspoken Lacey. Then there was Whizz, the guy who understood what she'd gone through, and didn't pressure her to change. She enjoyed being around him.

The café door opened, and she looked up to find Whizz making his way toward her. The scars on his face were fading, but they were there. Just like her own scars. She forced a smile, and went to stand when he shook his head.

"You're back so soon?" he asked.

"I had some things to do." She reached down into her bag and grabbed the envelope, handing it over to Whizz.

She sipped her coffee, watching as the waiter placed a hot coffee in front of Whizz. Licking her dry lips, she took another drink.

"This is a fantastic opportunity," Whizz said, folding up the letter and handing it back.

"Thanks."

"You took the interview?"

"I was there three hours ago."

"How did it go?"

"They offered me a job. I'm be a tech assistant, helping newbies, but they also showed me the ladder for promotion. They want to see what I'm capable of."

"I know you're damn good," Whizz said.

"Not as good as you."

"I'm an old guy, sweetie. I was around when computers were first invented."

She laughed at his joke. "You weren't, but I get what you're saying."

"Experience."

"Which is the key to everything, right?"

"Of course, it is," he said, drinking from his cup. "The question is, do you want to do this?"

She shoved the piece of paper back in her bag, and sighed. "I don't know what I want. It's hard."

"How are things going with you and Sinner?"

"Good. It's good."

"Only good," Whizz asked, sitting back, and folding his arms.

"He doesn't know about the interview today. I couldn't bring myself to tell him. Do you think that was wrong?"

"It doesn't matter what I think. You've got to think about yourself, Lola."

She stared across his shoulder out of the window. Sunlight was streaming in, and she loved summer time more than any other time of the year. She loved the warmth, the glow, the flowers, the love. All of it. There was no darkness in summer, and what was there, disappeared within a few hours. "There are times that I can't forget. I can't stop thinking that I'm still locked up waiting to die." She forced a smile, and hoped the tears that were filling her eyes disappeared.

"You're not dreaming, Lola. It has been years, and Andrew is long gone. Everyone associated with that monster is gone." Whizz reached out, putting a hand over hers.

"It still feels like it was yesterday." When a tear fell, she grabbed her tissues from her bag, and dabbed under her eyes. "I'm sorry."

"Don't be sorry. You don't have to ever worry about being yourself when you're with me." He patted her hand. "Have you spoken to Sinner about this?"

"No. Erm, he'll just … it's easier not to talk about it."

"Does he hurt you?"

"What? No, absolutely not. He just…" She didn't know what else to say. "He does everything for me. He's perfect in every single way."

"Why do I sense it's not what you want?" he asked.

"I don't know what I'm talking about to be honest." She went to take another sip of her coffee and found that it was in fact empty.

"This feeling you're getting, talk to Sinner. Tell him. See what he wants from you, and in return figure out what you want between the two of you."

She took a deep breath. "What if I need a break?"

"A break?"

"From Chaos Bleeds, from Piston County. From all of it. From MCs, and Sinner, and Andrew. Just to be able to be myself. God, I sound like a horrible person." She placed her head in her hands. "I don't want to hurt him, but I don't know anything else. I'm not fixed. I'm not broken. I'm damaged, Whizz. I'm … not good." She couldn't find the right words.

Silence fell between them, and when she had her emotions under control, she finally looked at him.

"You're hurting Sinner either way. With him, you're not whole, and you're not finding peace. Away from him, he's going to miss you. He loves you more than anything in the world. I can see that."

"I don't want to lose that. I love him, Whizz. I do. I just … ugh!" She growled. This was not helping. "I sound like a bitch, and I even hate that as well."

"Let's go for a walk." Whizz threw down some notes, and she followed him out of the café. Placing her bag on her shoulder, she folded her arms, and released another breath. The sun was warm and bright. Closing her eyes, she tilted her head up. "Come on."

She followed Whizz as they walked away from the café. When she had been recovering, before she went to Piston County, she used to take long walks with Angel, Lacey, and even Paris. They all allowed her time to think. During their visits for special occasions she would go for the same walks even in the snow and ice.

Walking helped to clear her head and to bring everything back into focus.

"You know what you want to do."

"I don't want to leave my family behind, Whizz."

"I know. You won't be. Do you want me to talk with Devil for you? Explain it?" he asked.

"No." They paused outside of a cemetery. She knew many of The Skulls were laid to rest there.

"This was where I met Lacey," Whizz said. "We had a freakish thing going in a graveyard."

"Spooky."

"Yeah. I was the scarred animal, and she was my princess. My inked princess. I found her, and she found me. Together we were broken, completely shattered apart, and little by little, we've been able to bring ourselves together, piece by aching piece."

"Are you trying to tell me that Sinner and I will do that for each other?"

"Sinner can help, but he's not broken, Lola. In your head, and in your heart, you're broken. You're not shattered anymore."

"I'm not going to talk to someone. That doesn't help."

"I'm not offering you the chance to talk to someone. I'm just telling you that I get it. You want out. You want to find yourself, and build yourself up." Whizz patted her arm. "There's no shame in that."

She expelled another breath. "What if he moves on, Whizz? I love him. I don't want to lose him."

"If he loves you, and you love him, you will find each other again. This is not going to be easy for you. It's going to fucking suck. There's no lying there. But *you* have to do what you need to do. No one else."

She licked her dry lips, and cursed the tears that once again started to fall. "I promised myself I wouldn't cry."

He chuckled. "Cry. It's a way of dealing, and you need to deal, honey. Are you coming back to my place? Lacey's ... actually, I really hope that Lacey is not cooking anything."

Lola burst out laughing. They all knew that Lacey was one of the worst cooks in the world.

"No, I've been away too long. I'm going to head back home before it's too late."

"Call me when you get home, Lola."

Chapter Two

Sinner glanced around the room of their apartment, and made sure everything was in place. He had been obsessing a little too much just lately. Lola didn't like mess, and he wasn't a big fan of it either. She had already called ahead to tell him she would be home, and not to worry. He *was* worried. He was fucking freaking out, and it was scaring the shit out of him.

No woman meant more to him than Lola. She had entered his world, turned it upside down, and now he couldn't for a second imagine life without her. Running a hand down his face, he went to the fridge and pulled out a beer. He'd not had a drink since the one that morning, and he wasn't an alcoholic. Just stressed.

Staring at the beer, he put it back in the fridge and settled on a coffee instead. He didn't have a problem, and right now, he wanted a clear head. When Lola came home, he wanted to clear the air, and make sure they were both on the same page when it came to their futures.

He had finished making his coffee when there was a knock on the door. It wasn't Lola. He could tell by the sound of the knock. Opening the door, he found Pussy on the other side.

"Hello, buddy. Long time, no see."

"Why are you here?" Sinner asked.

"Well, I've got a favor to ask. Do you want me to ask it here, or would you like me to invite me in? You know, what normal people do."

Sinner rolled his eyes, but opened his door a little wider.

"Good man," Pussy said, slapping his chest.

"What great favor do you need?" he asked.

"I'm taking Sasha out tomorrow night, and I was wondering how you felt to babysitting Shay?" Pussy asked, taking a seat. Sasha had once been blinded by her stepfather pushing her down a flight of stairs. The blow to the head had caused her blindness. The doctors had been convinced that she would see again, but it had never happened, until another blow had somehow brought her sight back. In the meantime, the dog that had been helping Sasha had been given back to help another person with sight difficulties. At the time, Sasha had been inconsolable, to the point that Pussy had demanded and paid a great deal to get the dog back. Ashley was now a retired guide dog.

"You want me to babysit your daughter."

"Of course. It would just be for the one night. You and Lola, together, what do you say?"

"What do I get out of it?" Sinner asked.

Pussy sighed. "You get the pleasure of babysitting my girl, and hopefully making your woman broody enough that you stop spilling all your problems at the clubhouse."

Sinner paused. "You knew about that?"

"Simon was telling everyone who would listen that you were having, air quote, 'girl troubles'." Pussy did the air quotes. "What's the deal?"

"You've only come to ask me so you could gossip behind my back."

"Yes and no. I want to take Sasha out, and I also need a babysitter. Devil told me I've used Lexie and Judi for the last time. Curse and Mia are having a family date. Death and Brianna told me no. Snake hissed at me. Dick told me to fuck off. Spider, well, he's got a plateful himself. With you and your girl troubles," he air quoted again, "I figured you'd be wanting all the help that you can get."

"I don't like you."

Pussy laughed. "You don't have to like me. I can live without being liked, baby. I just want you to watch Shay. Also, I think the only reason that everyone else has said no, and pretty much pointed me in your direction, the club feels you need this."

"The club needs me to look after your girl?"

"Yes. You'll be doing it for the club, and for Sasha."

"I do not want to know why Sasha needs it."

"You know why I got my nickname," Pussy said, to which Sinner groaned. "I'll give you a hint. It involves that."

"You're disgusting," Sinner said.

"You asked."

"What will it take to get rid of you?"

"Agree to look after Shay."

"Fine, fine. I'll do it. Just get out of my house before I throw up everywhere."

"Excellent." Pussy jumped up. "Just so you know, Lola has been waiting in her car for at least ten minutes that I knew of."

"What?"

"She was waiting in her car in the parking lot. Looked a little … strange."

"You didn't think to tell me this when you first arrived."

"Nope. I wanted you to look after my kid. Trouble in paradise."

"Go away, Pussy."

Pussy left his apartment, and Sinner moved toward the window, pulling back the curtain and seeing Lola's car parked where she normally left it. All the way up here, he couldn't see if she was still in the car. He watched as Pussy left the building, and didn't give any sign that Lola was still in the car. No wave, no acknowledgement.

Sinner turned about to head toward the car, when he saw Lola entering. She was dressed to impress in a pencil skirt, white blouse, with her black hair pinned back. She had once had brown hair, long lengths of it, but she had cut it off, and now had it dyed regularly.

"Hey," she said. "What did Pussy want?"

"We're babysitting tomorrow."

"Oh."

"He asked, and I wanted him gone. The only way to do that was to convince him that I would—"

"I get it. I do." She closed the door and flicked the lock. He watched as she removed her jacket and then the pins from her hair.

"Where were you today?" he asked, hating how he was feeling. He didn't want to be ordering her around, or forcing out answers. Why couldn't she just talk to him?

"I went to Fort Wills."

"Are we really going to do this, Lola?" he asked.

He watched as she paused, and nodded. "You know about the job interview."

"You had a reminder on your desk. You really didn't think I'd see."

"Yes, I had a job interview."

"It takes you away from Piston County."

"Yes."

"Away from us."

"What do you want me to say, Sinner? I don't … I don't know what to say to make this any better right now. There was a job interview. I went for it, and they even offered me the job."

"Did you take it?"

"I asked for time to think about it."

"So, you need to think about it?" he asked.

"Yeah, I did. I do."

He stared at her, and his heart was breaking. There was so much to say, and yet, he didn't have the first clue on what to do.

"Why don't we just cut the crap?" he asked. "You want to leave, don't you?"

He saw the tears in her eyes, and knew without a doubt that it was hurting her, just not as much as it was killing him. Sinner had known his feelings for her for a long time. He knew deep down in his heart that even as Lola wanted to love him, it was next to impossible to do so. They had to do this. *Lola* had to do this, even if it was killing him inside.

"I don't know what I want."

"You don't need to lie."

"I'm not lying, Sinner. Really, I'm not. I love what we have here. I love you, and I can't imagine being anywhere else. That is how much I love you."

"But?"

"It's not enough. Something is missing, and I don't want it to be like this."

"If you need to talk to someone, I can arrange it."

"No! I don't want to talk to anyone. I don't want to be coddled. I just … I want you to understand me."

"I can't understand you if you don't talk to me."

"I just can't do this anymore. I can't wake up and pretend that something isn't wrong. Let's face it, Sinner, every time you look at me, you see that broken little girl."

"No, I don't."

"Look around you!" She stomped her foot. "You make sure everything is spick and span. You won't allow me to clean up. There was a dog cage in the back of a truck, and you made me look elsewhere. You're coddling me, and you're not giving me the chance to grow."

"And you think this is the way to do that? To go out, and do this kind of shit?" He pointed at her clothes.

Silence fell between them.

Tears spilled down her cheeks, and he hated that he had been the cause.

"I didn't want this. I really didn't, but I can't keep living like this," she said. "I love you, but I have to go."

Sinner fisted his hands and gritted his teeth. He was breaking apart inside. "I want to help you, Lola. I love you."

"I know, but you can't help me. No one can help me, and it's only me. I've got to do this." She nibbled her lip. "There's not going to be anyone else. I love you."

"Are you asking me to wait for you?" Sinner asked. The thought of touching another woman repulsed him. His soul, his very essence belonged to her.

She sniffled. "I was hoping, but I can understand that it is just too much to ask for. I'm sorry." She stepped around him, and he closed his eyes.

There wasn't going to be any other woman. "You don't have to leave. I can go." He grabbed his jacket, and headed toward the door.

"I do love you, Sinner."

He stopped with his hand on the door. In all of his life, he had never once been so fucking broken. He couldn't help her.

"Just not enough."

Closing the apartment door didn't make him feel better. Nothing could ever make him feel better.

****

Packing up a suitcase didn't take long. Lola hadn't accumulated all that much in the past couple of years. It was pitiful what she did own, and there was no need for her to pack anything else. She made sure to take some pictures with her as well.

This was not what she wanted. She didn't want to lose Sinner, nor did she want to fight with him. She didn't know completely what she wanted, but it certainly wasn't this, and it was killing her.

He had looked so upset, so angry with her, and she hated it.

Wiping away the tears, in the back of her mind he could almost hear Andrew laughing at her. He'd been dead for a long time, and he was still mocking her, even from his grave.

Packing her car, she got behind the wheel, and drove all the way to Devil and Lexie's house. She knocked on the door, holding her laptop.

Devil answered wearing a pair of jeans and nothing else. "Lola, are you okay?"

"I'm fine. Can I speak with Lexie?"

"Yeah, sure, come in."

The moment she stepped through the door, she heard the screams and shouts of kids having fun. "It's movie night."

"I'm really sorry to barge in like this."

"It's fine." Devil walked into the kitchen, and that was where she found Lexie, who was dressed in shorts and a crop top. On her hip was Laurell.

"Hey, Lola." The moment Lexie looked at her, she handed off the baby and pulled her in for a hug. "What's going on?"

Devil must have left because he was no longer in the kitchen, and the kids had also gone quiet.

"He's taken them outside."

"I'm heading out for a while. There has been a job opportunity pop up, and I can't turn it down. I wanted to, but this needs to happen."

"What about Sinner?" Lexie asked.

She sighed. "It's over. We're over." Her lips wobbled. She felt another sob close to the surface, but she didn't cry. Instead, she took a deep breath, smiled, and handed Lexie the laptop.

"What's this?"

"This is everything, Lexie. Everything to do with Old Ladies MC. The website, and I've even left you a section on how to keep it updated. I've got to go."

Lexie took the laptop even as she shook her head. "You don't have to leave."

"I really do."

"What are you doing to do?" Lexie asked.

"I don't know. I just know that I can't do this anymore."

"You love Sinner?"

"More than anything. Something is missing, and I can't keep pretending that everything is fine." She shrugged. "I've got to head out, and I need to find myself."

"It's over?"

"Yeah, it has to be. I've got to go. I don't expect him to wait for me. I'd like him to. Believe me, I would really like him to, but I doubt it." She chuckled and wiped her eyes. "I've loved being here. I've loved being with all of you. You're my family, but I understand if you would like me to not return, and to keep my distance."

Lexie took hold of her hands. "Don't. You are welcome here. I get it, I do. I expect a phone call every single week. You hear? I want to make sure that you're fine. If you need money, call, and we will sort it out."

Once again, tears filled her eyes. "You're too good for me."

"You're family, Lola. Never forget that."

Lola said her good-byes and left. She had two

more stops to make. The first was to Natalie Pritchard. Lola had become friends with the rancher's daughter over the past few years. They had worked together on photography, getting the clothing store up and running. She had been the shoulder that Natalie had cried on, even when Slash was around. Lola was sure that Slash had a bit of a crush on Natalie, but she didn't say anything. She had never been able to read men, not even Sinner.

Driving down the long path, she felt her heart, little by little, breaking. These were her friends, and she loved them so much. Parking the car, she saw that Natalie was sitting on the porch steps with a drink in hand. Slash was also there, and he was doing some kind of dance that was making Natalie laugh.

The moment she pulled up, Natalie stood. Climbing out of her car, Lola forced a smile.

"Lola, what's up?" Natalie asked.

"Can we talk?"

"Sure, sure."

"That's my cue to leave." Slash didn't move toward his motorbike. No, he went inside Natalie's home.

"Is that new?" Lola asked.

"No, not really. Since my dad passed away, Slash has been sticking around lately. He doesn't like me being alone. Why are you here?" she asked.

"I'm heading out for a while."

Natalie stared at her. "Why do I feel this is going to mean something more?"

Lola took another deep breath, and explained in detail what had happened, and what she needed to do. Even as she was dealing with this decision, she hated it because it was hurting Sinner, but she had to do it.

"Wow, you're really going to go and do this?" Natalie asked.

"I don't have a choice. I need to do this." She thought about what Whizz said, and even as it was hurting her, she knew she was doing the right thing.

Natalie threw herself at Lola. "I'm going to miss you."

"You can call me. I'm not being blacklisted. That's what Lexie said. You have my cell phone."

"It's not going to be the same though, is it? You're going to be gone."

"I know, and I'm sorry. Really, I am. I don't want to cause anyone any kind of pain, but it doesn't matter because whatever I do will cause it." She hugged Natalie close. "I love you, sweetie. Keep doing what you do, and you're going to rock everything."

"It's not going to be the same without you."

She held onto Natalie tightly, and forced herself to get back into her car, and to start the journey toward Paris.

Lola wasn't surprised to see Paris waiting for her. "You're leaving."

"I'm leaving." She ran fingers through her hair. "Who told you?"

"Lexie. She thought it would be good for me to know in advance. Spider is looking after Aria."

Aria was Paris's little girl.

"I'm sorry."

Paris sighed. "I thought there was something wrong. I figured you would come and talk to me." She walked down the steps toward her. With each step, Lola was sure she heard her future being rewritten, as if that could make any sense to her. She could stay or go. "It's him, isn't it? Andrew. You've got to do something about it."

"I need to find my way."

"And your way is not here with people who love

you."

"I love you all so much. You know that, and I would do anything for all of you. I don't want to hurt anyone. I really don't."

"It has been years," Paris said.

"I'm not like you, Paris. I talked to the doctors, I said the right things, and I do everything that makes it look like I'm fine. For a long time, I thought I could convince myself that I'm happy, that I'm better."

"You weren't?"

Lola shook her head. "I've never been right, Paris. I'm not as strong as you."

"Don't do that. You're a strong woman. Like you said, everyone handles themselves differently." Paris hugged her like she had many times before. "Just know that I'm going to worry about you."

"Lexie has already told me that I've got to keep in touch."

"You should. None of us would expect anything else. You've got to keep in touch, and tell us what you're doing, and how you're getting on. We all love you, Lola. We all will miss you."

Lola sighed. "Thank you. For everything."

"We're friends. It's what friends do."

Paris gave her a final squeeze, and that was it. Without looking back, Lola climbed into her car, and drove away. She got to the border of Piston County, and for an hour, maybe even longer, she stared at the sign. Her heart was in this small MC run town. Chaos Bleeds controlled everything. They were not cruel, or malicious.

Chaos Bleeds had a love that very few could ever contemplate, and for a short time she was part of it.

You need to do this.
Make yourself better.
Fix yourself.

With that, she drove out of Piston County, and for the first time in her life, she felt hope.

Chapter Three

Going back to their apartment was the worst. Sinner didn't believe he could feel any kind of pain worse than seeing her half of the closet empty. Lola was gone, and instead of being understanding, he had sent her off in anger. He'd been angry, and she had wanted to talk, and he didn't want to deal with knowing she was going. Lola had to go. That night, he'd not slept, and instead had spent the entire night staring down at a picture of the two of them together.

Lola was the bar of soap, and he had squeezed her too tightly. He had completely fucked everything up, and it was his fault.

Within twenty-four hours the entire club knew, and they all looked at him, clearly expecting him to freak out or have a problem. Instead, he kept on working. The hours turned into days, and the days into weeks. He didn't stop to think, and he kept on working.

Dividing his time between Naked Fantasies, Old Ladies MC clothing, and Natalie's ranching fields, every time he got back to the clubhouse he was exhausted. For an entire month he did that, and he stopped going home.

Their apartment sat, waiting for someone to come back, and he couldn't do it. He couldn't go back there. Sinner was aware of Lola being in touch with Lexie and Paris. She probably was talking with Whizz, but he didn't talk to them.

The thing Sinner hated most was their pitying gazes.

Into the second month, with summer fading fast and fall upon them, he sat on the clubhouse wall, watching the party going on all around them. The Skulls were present, and in the corner, Simon and Tabitha were talking. The other kids were playing around on the little park they had set up. The two clubs mingled like they were old friends.

"Hello," Angel said, coming toward him.

He smiled at Lash's old lady.

"Hey, Angel."

"You look so sad," Angel said, taking a seat beside him.

"I've not got a lot to smile about these days."

"Whizz told us what happened." Angel tucked some of her blonde hair behind her ear. She had gone through a stage of dyeing it. Lacey was a beautician, or something to do with hair and beauty. She experimented on all of the old ladies, and the club whores, not that there were many of them.

He hadn't been interested in women.

It was stupid. He had told Lola he wouldn't wait, and yet, it was all lies. There was no way that he could touch another woman.

"Yeah, well, everyone knows."

"She's doing okay. In case you were interested."

He paused in drinking his beer, and turned toward her.

"I know you've not asked Lexie or anyone else. I thought you would like to know."

Sinner stared at his drink and shook his head. "I do, and I don't."

"You're angry with her?" Angel asked.

"Yeah, I'm angry with her. I love her more than anything, and she has just walked away. Pretended that we've not got anything going on."

Angel held his hand. "It'll be okay."

Lash appeared, gripping Angel's shoulder, and kissing her head.

Sinner pulled his hand away. Angel was an old

lady who really believed in kindness and love. She always tried to make someone feel part of their world. Sinner smiled. "Thank you, Angel."

"She does love you," Angel said.

"Enjoy the party." He nodded at Lash, and made his way into the kitchen. Lexie was there, dabbing barbeque sauce onto racks of ribs. She smiled at him. "How is she?"

"It has taken you a month to ask that."

"I'm being an asshole, I know, but please, tell me if she's okay."

Lexie put the saucepan down and turned toward him. "Yes, she's fine. She's got a little apartment in the city, and she's working in a technology firm. She talks nonstop about that, and to be honest, I don't have the first clue what she's saying. She's made some friends."

"Is there another guy?"

"No. She doesn't talk about anyone."

Sinner nodded. "I've got to go."

"Sinner, you don't have to leave. Why don't you call her?" Lexie asked. "You're both hurting."

"She left, Lexie. She left me, and I'm not … I'm not going to force her to do something she doesn't want to do."

"Even if she does love you?" Lexie asked.

He laughed. "She loves me. Everyone keeps telling me that."

"Then why do you doubt it?"

"Would you dream of leaving Devil to go and find yourself?" he asked but didn't give her the chance to answer. "What about Angel and Lash? Tiny and Eva? What about fucking Simon and Tabitha? Huh? What about them? They're fucking kids, and even with cities apart, or clubs apart, they still find the time for each other."

Devil stepped into the kitchen.

Sinner had gone from talking to yelling, his anger consuming him.

"I wish people would not tell me that she fucking loves me. She loves me, I get it. She just doesn't love me enough."

"I think we need to talk," Devil said.

"Are you going to tell me that she loves me, too?" Sinner asked, unable to keep the sneer out of his voice.

"No. I'm not. I'm not going to tell you bullshit that you don't want to hear." Devil stepped up close to him. "Yelling at my woman though, you know I don't like that."

Sinner sighed and followed Devil back to his office. There was a door leading toward where they held church, making decisions for the good of the club.

"I'm sorry," Sinner said.

"Chaos Bleeds has a Nomad Chapter. A select group of men who cannot settle down. Adam was part of The Skulls. They don't play a part in club messes, but when needed, they come running."

"I know of the Nomad Chapter."

"I want you to think about this, Sinner." Devil stared at him.

"You want me gone?"

"You're working yourself into the ground. I know what you need more than anything. What I'm reminding you, is there is a chance for you to clear your head. No commitments. Piston County holds a shitload of memories for you. Everywhere you turn, you can remember her. You've not been back to your apartment, and I don't even want to think of the state of the place."

"Everyone is telling me how much she loves me."

"And you're sick of it. I'm not going to assume that she loved you, Sinner. I didn't know her that well to tell you if she did. If you want me to hold your hand, and treat you like a fucking girl, I'll do it. I love my men, all of you. You know that. This what you've got going. I don't like it. It's not good for the club, and it's not good for you. Forget about Lola. Think about yourself."

Devil slapped him on the back.

"That is it?" Sinner asked.

"Yeah. You're already hurt, Sinner. I can only imagine what it's like having everyone tell me that my woman loves me, especially if she's not around. This time, you get a freebie, but don't let it happen again."

****

"I think we need to get a drink, and get laid," Sarah said.

Lola finished what she was doing, and logged off her computer, turning to her friend. Sarah was a pretty woman who demanded that they go out every single Friday night. No matter the occasion, Sarah loved to party.

Lola hated partying.

"Are you going to take up some of the men on their offer?" Belinda asked, leaning in close to her.

Belinda and Sarah were two women Lola had become friends with. Well, "friends" was too strong a word. They were acquaintances.

"I'm not ready to date," Lola said. In her heart and mind she was still taken. Lexie had told her that Sinner still wasn't dating anyone else. Still, she didn't know what to expect.

Have you made a mistake?

"Lola, honey, you can't be miserable forever," Sarah said. "You've got to live a little."

"We'll see. I've got to go and change, okay? I'll meet you back at the bar. Our regular place?"

"Yes, sure."

Lola didn't stick around. She made her way out of the building and went straight to her apartment. She lived five minutes away. Since leaving Piston County she had done more in the way of walks than when she lived in a small town. She loved the hustle and bustle of the city, the chaos of it.

Entering her apartment, she made herself a sandwich, and called Lexie's number.

Her friend answered on the second ring.

"Hey, honey. You doing okay?" Lexie asked.

In the background, she heard what sounded like partying. "I'm doing great. What's happening there?"

"Oh, we've got some of The Skulls here. We're enjoying the last few rays of sunshine while we can. How are you?"

"I'm fine. You know. Doing well."

"That's good."

"How is Sinner?" she asked.

"Lola, I'm not going to get in the middle of this, but what and how do you think he's feeling? He's hurt, okay?" Lexie sighed. "Don't keep asking about him. You're not going to like the answers, honey."

The sandwich she had been eating no longer appealed. "You're right, and I'm sorry."

"Me too. I can't stay and chat. Love you, Lola."

Before she could say anything else, Lexie hung up. Staring at her cell phone, Lola let out a breath. Tears were so close to the surface that she could taste them.

Pulling up Sinner's name on her cell phone, she stared at it, wondering what the hell she was to do. Nothing was helping her. Not work, not her new friends, which she thought about as anything but.

The apartment was nice, small, and empty. Her whole life was one big fat empty, and yet she just knew that she wasn't done yet. She wasn't finished doing what she was going to do.

Closing her phone, she placed it on the counter, and went to her bathroom. She took a long shower in an attempt to clear her thoughts that were nothing but a jumbled mess inside her head. Nothing made sense to her. Not what she wanted. Not what she was looking for. Everything was just shit in her head, and nothing made sense. Not one thing.

She didn't spend too much time getting ready. Jeans and a shirt that revealed some cleavage were all that she allowed herself. A slight heel, minimal makeup, her hair pulled back, and she was done. She had never spent all that much time on her appearance. It had never felt necessary, not at all.

Leaving her apartment, she walked toward the nightclub where her friends would be. The bouncer, Harold, let her in. She had helped him set up his child's laptop while he was on break last week. Since then, he had been nice to her, helping her out.

Entering the nightclub, at first she was overcome by how many people were there.

"By the time I'm through with you, you'll never forget me."

Pushing Andrew's voice away, she forced herself to take each step toward the bar. She took a seat, and wasn't surprised to find Sarah and Belinda already on the dancefloor, partying it up.

She wondered what it was like back at Piston County, loving life, and dancing around, all of that shit.

Ordering herself a drink, she sat at the bar and watched everyone around her. The barman handed her a bottle of water and a straw. She unscrewed the lid, placed the straw inside, and took a drink. Each movement was meticulous so she didn't get anything wrong or screw up. No one tampered with her drink. She had pepper spray, and her keys, which were deadly.

"You know, I've seen you here every Friday for the past three weeks, and you never talk to anyone. The men who try to chat you up end up with their tail between their legs. So, I'm going to see if I can change that, princess."

"Don't call me that," she said, turning to her right and finding a very handsome man taking a seat beside her.

The guy held his hands up. "I'm sorry. I'm just curious why a pretty girl such as yourself is here in this bar if you're not interested in the entertainment."

She sipped at her drink, wondering if she ignored him long enough, he'd leave.

He didn't.

"The name's Chris—"

"I'm taken," she said, turning to him. "I'm actually the old lady of an MC member."

Chris went pale. "If that's true, why are you here?"

"Because I just want to enjoy a drink. Leave me alone."

Without another word, Chris whoever got up and left.

****

"Today was a good day," Devil said.

"Yeah, it was. Did you see Simon and Tabitha? They were so cute, and he gave her those chocolates me made."

Devil groaned. "Could you not remind me? Why do they get to be cute?"

"They're kids, and it's cute to watch them. They are going to end up together. I've told you this numerous times. Accept it, move on, and deal with something else."

"You mean the depressing issue of Lola and

Sinner?"

Lexie sighed. She was rubbing moisturizing cream into her hands as she moved toward the bed. Devil put the book he was reading down on the drawer beside their bed. She knelt down beside him, moving so that her back was to him, and she snuggled in. "I kind of lost my temper on the phone today. She asked about him."

"I get angry, babe, thinking about them. They clearly love each other, and she's gone off to fucking soul search, and Sinner's just waiting. I don't like it."

"We knew something like this would happen," Lexie said. "I don't know what to think anymore. I mean, I get that Lola went through so much, but it was years ago now. They were getting better."

"I spoke with Whizz about it before he headed out. I just didn't understand you know? How can one minute she seem fine, and the next minute, be leaving. You know?" he asked.

"Yeah, I do. What did he say?"

"He reckons that unlike Paris, Lola didn't deal with it. She just pushed it to one side, and ignored it. Falling in love with Sinner helped her to keep on ignoring it. Shit just got worse though." Devil kissed her neck. "I want to help them."

"Did you give Sinner the option of going to the Nomad Chapter?" she asked.

"I did. I don't know if he'll take it or not."

"Do you think he's overreacting?"

"Babe, if it had been you, I would have taken your ass back."

"But I've not been through what Lola's been through," Lexie said. "God, it's easy to ignore all the crap. Between the kids, the businesses, and the club, I was able to forget about everything we've faced over the years." She sighed, placing her hands over his where he held her. "Simon's getting older, and in a few years, he's going to be causing so much trouble of his own."

"Please, don't remind me. I'm terrified. Elizabeth is getting cocky, and what am I going to do with guys start calling for her?" Devil asked.

"I know how it should go," Lexie said, laughing.

"I've got a special gun for all guys that think they can come around for Elizabeth and Laurell. I hate men."

"Baby, you're one of them." Lexie tried to soothe him.

"I know. Why do you think I know what I want to do to all the guys? I have a firsthand knowledge of all of the sick shit going through their heads, and believe me when I say, it isn't pretty." He hugged her a little tighter. "Just think of all the things I still want to do to you. Just watching you bend down, and I get hard as fucking rock."

Her pussy went slick thinking about it. The one thing she missed most was the time alone they used to get. Five kids down the line and they had to pay a babysitter, or get one of the brothers to do it.

Judi would it without hesitation, but she had two kids already and didn't need the extra fuss.

"We're still no closer to figuring out what we're going to do," Lexie said.

"We'll do what we have to do, baby."

"Do you know what is going to happen?" she asked.

"I don't have a fucking clue."

There was a knock on their door. Devil called for whoever it was to enter. Simon was there. He was in a pair of pajama bottoms. "Daddy, look at my muscles," he said, flexing them.

"You are big and strong, son."

"Can I go to weight training?" Simon asked.

"Weight training?" This time Lexie was confused. "You're eight."

"Yeah, but I want to start now. I want to be big and strong so I can protect my girl, Tabby. Tiny said only a big strong man with muscles the size of elephants was going to marry his girl. I've got to get them! Dad, please."

Lexie burst out laughing. Devil kissed her head. "Remind me the next time I'm with Tiny that I'm going to beat the shit out of him."

She watched as her husband took Simon back to his room, probably to have a long talk. She couldn't help but adore the budding relationship between her Simon and Tabitha. It was a romance that was going to be epic.

Chapter Four

Two months later

"You're sure about this?" Devil asked.

"I'm sure. It's time for me to do something. I can't sit around all day." Sinner placed the apartment key on the desk. "I'm not quitting the club. I just need some fresh air. You know. I need to bring shit back into focus. This was what you offered me. I'm taking you up on that."

"I'm not going to lie, it's going to be sad to see you go." Devil moved from behind his desk, and leaned against it.

Sinner glanced around the office. "I never thought I'd leave Piston County."

"You're going to need a patch." Devil grabbed the one that Sinner had already spotted. "Here you go. You okay to stitch it on?"

"Yeah, I can stitch on the patch." He glanced down at the two words, Nomad Chapter. His leather jacket already had Chaos Bleeds on it. Now he had to include that he was part of the Nomads.

"There's no Prez there. You're a band of brothers. I called to Lucius. He's put the word out about you becoming a Nomad. Remember, you can stop here any chance you want. We're still your family, and I'll make sure your apartment is taken care of."

Sinner nodded. "Thanks for this."

"Is she worth this?" Devil asked.

"You know, I thought about that. I even watched one of the club whores. For a split second, I thought about getting over Lola by having another woman. I couldn't do it. I don't want anyone else. I guess for the right woman, you just know. I've stared at my cell phone more often that I could count. All it would take was one phone call."

"Then why don't you phone her? If you ask her, I imagine she'd come to you. She does love you in her way."

"In her way, yeah, exactly. She's going to come to me because I ask her to, and I don't want that. I want her to do what she needs to do, and I'm going to be ready for her."

"You're still going to take her back after everything?" Devil asked.

Sinner smiled. "Of course, I am. First, I'm going to get my shit together. Like Lexie said, I squeezed too tightly, and in doing so, I caused this just as much as she did. We made mistakes. I have no doubt that we're going to find each other again. That's just not going to happen right now." He held out his hand waiting for Devil.

Devil shook his head. "You're a fine man, Sinner."

"You betcha ass I am." He winked at Devil. He was feeling better in his own mind. He and Lola had needed this break more than anything. From the moment, they had settled down in Piston County, it had been one fucking thing after another. They hadn't been able to sit back, and bask in settling down. In doing so, he'd changed. He knew that. He wasn't the same man that he'd been just eight years ago.

It was hard to think that eight years ago, they'd come to Piston County where Simon was housed with his auntie Lexie.

Leaving the office, he saw several of the guys had lined up to wish him well, Pussy, Ripper, Curse, Dime, Slash, Reese, Charlie, just to name a few.

He got to his bike, and that was where he saw Butler. "You're not going to come with me?"

Butler looked at the patch and shook his head. "I can't leave. Being on the road, it held too much temptation. I don't want to open that door again. I'm clean, and I'm happy about that."

Sinner saw that his friend was struggling, and he hated that fact that he even asked. "I'm sorry, man."

"I know, and I'm sorry." Butler ran fingers through his hair. "Life on the road, it's hazy, you know. Being clean, it has become my whole life, and I don't want to lose that."

"You're strong, man. I don't think you'll ever cave to that old shit."

Butler held his arms out. "I'm not even going to give it a chance. I wish you the best, and I hope more than anything that you find what you're looking for."

Within minutes Sinner was on his bike, and out of the clubhouse. The open road. There was no looking back, only going forward. He rode for over an hour, not caring where he was going in any direction. He had the clothes on his back, with his wallet, patch, and a few bare essentials. Part of being on the open road was not having any shit wearing him down. It was all about the freedom.

After riding for three hours straight, he pulled off at a café that looked like it had seen better days. Parking his bike, he took a seat, giving his order to the waitress, who again had seen better days. Taking out his stitching kit, he pulled his leather jacket off, and began to stitch on the patch.

He didn't pay any attention to the waitress as she brought him coffee and food. In between working the patch onto his leather jacket, he ate, drank, and smoked. No one tried to stop him. This was his domain.

Sinner held his jacket up, assessing his work. It wasn't perfect, but it would do. Chaos Bleeds Nomad Chapter.

"Are you all done?" the woman, Trisha, asked.

"Yeah, I'll have another coffee."

She grabbed his plates and empty cups. "You know a few of you boys were here the other day. You're a little behind."

"Sweetheart, we don't always ride together. Were they Chaos Bleeds?"

"Jacket said so. I don't really pay much attention. All sorts come through here. You're all the same."

Sinner smirked. There it was, the judgment. In a weird kind of way, it felt good to be judged again. "Oh, lady, if only you knew what I could get up to." He gave her a wink, and she snorted.

"Son, you don't even know what danger is." She waved her hand as if he was nothing more than a child.

It felt good to be back, and that was exactly how he felt. Back.

****

"He left?" Lola asked.

"I'm sorry, honey. You couldn't expect Sinner to wait around for you. He needed some air."

"It's fine. I just, the Nomad Chapter? I've never heard of them?" Lola rubbed her head, trying to figure out why she didn't know anything about another chapter of Chaos Bleeds.

"Why would you? You have met a couple of guys from the Nomad Chapter. Truth be told, there's not a lot to tell. They are ... dangerous. They're part of Chaos Bleeds, but they don't stick to a clubhouse, and they don't see themselves as controlled. If Devil needs them, he'll ask them, but again, there's not always a guarantee that they'll turn up."

"Why are they part of Chaos Bleeds?"

"Before Devil came to town, they all rode together for some time. The men consider themselves part of the Chaos Bleeds crew. I believe there is also a crew for The Skulls. Adam was part of it."

Lola knew Adam, and sighed. "Is there any way of getting in touch with him?"

"You've not spoken to him up to now, Lola."

"He didn't call me either." She felt ... defensive.

"Why should he? *You* left. Oh, honey, I don't want to fight, okay? I'm tired, and fighting is not what I want to do right now. You knew something like this would happen, and guess what? It has."

Lola heard the exhaustion in Lexie's voice. "You're completely right. So, what's been happening at home?"

"Everything is going okay. Judi is pregnant with baby number three. We also got the news that Dick and Martha are pregnant for the first time. We're going to be having a big baby shower for the two."

"I will try and make it back home. When will it be?"

The date was in three months' time.

"Mommy, Josh spat on my card again. It has to be perfect for Tabby," Simon said in the background.

"I'll let you go."

"Bye, Lola."

The call ended, and she stared down at her cell phone. Lexie had started to grow bored of talking to her, and Lola couldn't blame her. Even Paris had stopped calling. Glancing around her apartment, she sat back, and just stared. Sinner was on the road, and there was only one way of getting in touch with him. That was calling him.

It was so hard to just call him, and it drove her crazy. It shouldn't be hard at all. They'd had a life together, which she had ruined because she felt the need to.

There was a knock at the door, and she hadn't been expecting any guests. Getting up from the sofa took a lot of work, and she didn't want to talk to anyone.

Opening the door, she saw that Lacey was on the other side with Sally and Daisy.

"Oh, wow, I had no idea you were coming here," Lola said, opening up her door.

"Last time I checked there was nothing wrong with having a girly Friday night. Please tell me you don't have plans with those awful women?"

"Sarah and Belinda? No, they stopped inviting me. According to them, having a friend sitting at the bar all night, refusing offers of dancing is just too embarrassing. So, here I am."

"Lucky for you, we have guy trouble." Lacey pointed at Sally.

"This is not about me, Mom. This is about you. She's having a fight with Whizz."

"Mommy and Daddy are fighting about food," Daisy said, rushing to sit down, and already had the television on.

"I may have accidentally set our kitchen on fire."

"There was no accident about it, Mom. You totaled the kitchen," Sally said.

Lola looked toward the kitchen to see Sally rummaging around her fridge. It had been a couple of years since the attack on The Skulls clubhouse had taken Sally's leg from then knee down. She now wore a prosthetic, and she had trained nonstop to make sure she could walk without fault. At the end of long days, she was always in pain.

"How did you total the kitchen?" Lola asked, taking a seat beside Daisy.

"I turned my back."

Lacey said nothing else.

"She left the oven on. A pan of water burned dry, but she also placed a towel on the stove, forgetting about it. That towel was spread out, onto a newspaper. As you can imagine, one set fire to the other, and then the kitchen went up in flames," Sally said, making up some sandwiches as she did. "Ergo, Dad's pissed, and Mom has decided to have a girly day with you, while trying to make out it is about me."

Daisy nudged her. "Drew has told Sally that he loves her, and we all know Steven loves her."

"Drew didn't say that. He simply told me that without me, he wouldn't have been able to deal. It's only because my injury was worse than his," Sally said, coming into the sitting room. She handed out some sandwiches, and Lola took hers gratefully. Sally lowered herself down into a chair, and it was then that Lola saw the perspiration on her forehead. "Nothing will ever happen between me and Drew. He's a friend."

"That's because you love Steven." Daisy drew out the word love.

Lacey sat on the edge of the sofa with all of her ink on glorious display. She wore a shirt and a pair of jeans, which showcased all of her curves. To Lola, Lacey was one of the most beautiful women she had seen. Going through hell and back, she had a wit and fire about her.

"You don't mind me crashing here, do you?" Lacey asked.

"Not at all. I'd be glad of the company. I had some upsetting news."

"Oh—"

"We'll talk when the little one is in bed."

Sally's cell phone went off, and Lola watched the other girl's face transform.

"Thank you," Lacey said. "I don't like fighting

with Whizz."

"Especially when you're wrong," Sally said.

"I thought you were on my side?"

"There is no side, Mom. It's simple. You fucked up, and Dad freaked." Sally tilted her head to the side. "Do you even know why he freaked?"

"He was angry that I had been in the kitchen. He has put a weird ban on it."

"It was a necessary ban," Sally said. "You can't cook, and you nearly served raw chicken."

"It said it was cooked."

"It was white on the outside, and pink in the center. You cannot cook. Besides, Dad was pissed because you could have hurt yourself, and us. He was worried, and you acted like a bitch."

Daisy gasped. "We can't tell Mom that. Dad told us we have to keep it a secret."

Lola laughed as Lacey huffed. "I'm not in the wrong."

"Maybe you're a little in the wrong," Lola said. "I don't mind. I get to have some company." She rested her head on Lacey's shoulder, needing someone.

"Whizz sends his love."

"And you don't mind that."

"Honey, if I was worried, I wouldn't be telling you. I know that Whizz loves me."

They sat watching some weird cartoon. Sally's cell phone kept on dinging in between, and Lola was content. She had her friends, and right now, she couldn't break apart, not even if she wanted to. She had friends, guests, and she was going to make sure she didn't spoil their time.

After food, they bathed and put Daisy to bed. Lola went to the fridge, and decided to open that bottle of wine that she had been putting off.

She poured three large glasses, and sat down on the sofa. Sally took the wine, and sipped at it.

"How are you?" Lola asked.

"I'm fine. Ignore what Daisy said. Drew and I are friends. I wouldn't even dream of pretending to be anything else."

"You love Steven?"

Sally's cheeks went bright red, and she rubbed her temple. "That's even more complicated."

"Why?"

"I don't know. Maybe because I'm younger than he is."

"So, Sinner's older than me." Lola shrugged. "I didn't leave because of our ages."

"Why did you leave?" Sally asked. "I thought you were happy that you were getting better?"

"I thought I was, but guess what? I lied." Lola laughed, even though humor was the furthest thing from her mind. "Looking back over the past couple of months, I don't know why I left. Isn't that a nightmare scenario right now?" She sighed. "I wasn't happy, and Sinner, he was … so overprotective. I know that seems crazy, but he was protecting me all the time. He was making sure nothing hurt me, or that anyone didn't push too hard." She ran fingers through her hair. "It wasn't right. I didn't want him to always be protecting me. I love him so much, and don't you think he should be free to do that? Not worry about me all the time." Tears filled her eyes, and she sighed. "Ignore me. I suck."

"You don't suck, Lola. It will be okay."

"I don't think it will be."

"You don't?" Lacey asked, slumping down beside her, and taking her glass from the coffee table.

"I've just called Lexie before you turned up. Sinner's left Piston County. He's on the road, and there's nothing I can do about that. I may never see him again." The tears that had been swimming in her eyes, cascaded down her cheeks. She hated crying so much and would usually do anything to avoid crying.

"Oh, honey," Lacey said, hugging her close. "Does he still have his cell phone?"

"Yes, but should I call him? I was wrong to do this."

"You had your reasons. We won't all get it or understand why you did it. You may not see this, but you're drinking wine, and you didn't freak out when I knocked on the door. You're stronger than you were three months ago. This life away from both clubs, and working, and being with those two loser friends, has helped you."

Lola laughed. "How can you make me feel so good?"

"Because I've been where you are. I'm here now, with the love of my life pissed that I could have killed myself."

"Did you really total your kitchen?"

"She did," Sally said. "It's going to stink, badly."

"Whizz is already dealing with the repairs," Lacey said. "This is not about us, honey. This is about you."

"I want Sinner, but I want him when I can be myself. Pre-Master, not post-Master." She shook her head. "If that is even possible."

"How about you just become you, and you don't try to be the old you? Be the new you. I had to." Sally pointed at her leg. "I'm not the old me. I could sit and wallow in what I lost, and I lost something. Or I could keep moving forward. That's what you need to do, Lola, move forward. If you love Sinner and you don't want to lose that, call him." Sally held out Lola's cell phone.

"Sometimes, couples need distance to make the heart grow stronger, and others need time. You're not like every other couple. You may not be perfect this year, or next year, but one day soon, I think you would find yourself with him again."

Silence fell in the room.

"I think you need to take a career in writing romance," Lacey said. "That was so sweet."

Sally chuckled. "It's the happily-ever-afters that get me. I just want everyone to have theirs. Is that too much to ask?"

"In this day and age, it certainly seems it."

Lola stared down at her cell phone, and she didn't know what to do.

"Sally, why don't we get changed for bed, and give Lola some privacy?"

Lacey and Sally left her alone, and pushing her hair out of her face, Lola stared down at the phone. One phone call was all it took.

She tapped at her phone, bringing up Sinner's name.

This was her chance of doing this.

Don't back down.

Don't fight this.

Tapping his name, and held the cell phone to her ear.

I can do this.

For the longest time the phone rang, and rang, and rang. Once again, she felt her heart was being torn in two, but it was all her fault.

She waited to see if he would answer, hoping that he would, praying that he would.

Her wishes were answered.

"Lola," he said.

Just hearing his voice had her crying out.

"Sinner. I love you so much. God, why did I wait to call you?" She covered her mouth, and tried to stop the sobbing. It was just too much. She needed to hear his voice, to know that he was doing okay. She missed him so much.

"I love you, too, baby. What's wrong?" Sinner asked.

"I heard what happened. You leaving Chaos Bleeds. You're on the road."

"I had to clear my head."

"I'm so sorry I hurt you."

"I'm not going to say that it didn't hurt me. It did, and you know what, it's a good thing. I've been able to see where I fucked up."

"Oh, Sinner, you never fucked up. I swear. This is all me."

"It's not. I promise, babe. I needed this as much as you."

"You're on the road?" she asked.

"I've stopped for the night. Checked into a motel. I have to say, this place is really fucking shitty. I don't think they've changed the bedding, but it's a nice warm bed."

She chuckled. "You did say you loved being on the road and how unpredictable it can be."

"Yeah, I'm not seeing the appeal right now. It's good to hear your voice, baby."

The way he said "baby" gave her a thrill that she hadn't experienced in a long time. Closing her eyes, she released a sigh. "You know what to do and say to get me all warm inside."

"I wish you were here right now. What are you wearing?" he asked.

She glanced down at her jeans and shirt. "Nothing."

"The things I'd do to you right now would have you screaming my name in seconds."

She gritted her teeth. "Lacey, Sally, and Daisy are here. Can we take a rain check for tomorrow? I'll call you?"

"You got it, babe."

"Will you always get into a motel?"

"Nope. Sometimes it'll just be me and the stars."

It sounded wonderful.

"I love you, Sinner."

"Thank you for calling me, Lola."

They said their good-byes, and she stared down at her cell with a smile. Maybe, just maybe she'd be able to find her way back to him.

Chapter Five

Sinner didn't wait around for long, and the next morning before dawn, he was out of the motel and on the road again. He would need to pick up an odd job in a week as his money had all but dried up. If he became too strapped for cash, he'd call Devil, but part of the thrill of being on the road was living day to day.

That night he was excited about. Lola had called him, and she had promised to call him again tonight. He wanted to find another motel to be able to take that call, or at least a secluded spot that was peaceful.

He saw a biker pit stop within thirty minutes, and he pulled up. Filling up his bike, he headed inside the small diner, and burst out laughing.

"You've got to be shitting me," he said.

"Sinner, my man. Devil said you were on the road, but I couldn't believe it." Lucius got up from his seat, and pulled him in for a hug.

Lucius wasn't alone either. Sinner clocked several of the Nomad Chapter in residence. "Is this a party that I wasn't invited to?"

"We're banding together for a couple of weeks. We go up and down the coast, partying, and bringing joy to virgin pussies," Lucius said. "You're more than welcome to join. There's seven of us right now. You know that's not all of us. I heard that Crow had gone to find his soul or some shit. Redemption he's after."

Crow was a troubled brother. He had a kill list that was bigger than any club's combined. For the longest time, Crow had been coveted by several MCs, Trojans and Dirty Fuckers MC, included. As it was, Crow had wanted Chaos Bleeds, as they had been the only club who hadn't wanted him.

He had been living in Piston County so long that he had lost connection to his other brothers. Not all of the Chaos Bleeds crew settled down in one place.

Sinner looked at the men, and nodded. "Why not, but I've got to take a phone call tonight."

"Whatever, dude. We've got some bitches along for the ride. They make the journey more than fun."

As if on cue, six women came out of the toilet. They were dressed to impress. They didn't look like club whores, but something more.

"They travel with us. They have the wanderlust, and have defied the odds," Lucius said.

They took a seat a little away from the group that was causing a stir.

"Devil gave me a bit of the lowdown on your situation. You okay?" Lucius asked.

"Yeah, I'm fine. This is not going to be permanent." Sinner took a cigarette out of the packet, and lit it up. "I've got plans, and as much as I'm loving this, I just, I can't give up the life I've made for myself."

"I love Devil, man, I really do. He's the Prez of all Prez's. I don't know how you can do it. Sit down, and watch life pass you by. There's too much pussy available to give it up." Lucius took a long draw on his cigarette. "I didn't think this shit in Piston County would last. Just goes to show that a good pussy can keep a man locked up tight."

"You've not seen Devil and Lexie together."

"Don't need to. I've heard enough, and he sends me pictures all the time." Lucius pulled out his cell phone and brought them up. "I know they're all cute, but this guy here, he's going to be trouble." He pointed at Simon.

"That kid there is so damn smart," Sinner said. Seeing some of the pictures reminded him of what he'd

SAM CRESCENT

left behind. "You really don't want to settle down? Have a family?"

Lucius shook his head. "Nope. Not going to happen. I don't want any brats, any bitches. The open road is all I want. I've got one life, and I intend to live it the way I want. By the time I get back to heaven or hell, my body is going to be well used."

Sinner laughed.

Lucius was a hard ass through and through. He had nothing to live for, and nothing to lose, which made him dangerous.

"What did surprise me was Dick. That man is not friendly, and yet he's married and having a kid now I hear," Lucius said.

"He surprised the whole of the club. Martha's a good woman. All of the old ladies are good women. They have their moments, but for all intents and purposes they've made us better. We're better for having them in our lives."

"You can hear it."

Sinner stared down at the table. He ran his fingers down an old knife mark. It had been well worn so that it was no longer rough around the edges.

"You're looking a little sad there, Sinner. You ride with us, we have one demand, and that is you've got to be happy. You're not happy and I'm going to have a few issues with that."

Sinner laughed. "Don't worry about me. I won't be fucking anything, but I know how to party."

"You're pussy-whipped?"

"I'm pussy-whipped, and we're on a much-needed break," Sinner said. Regardless of what others thought, he wasn't going to be stepping out on his woman.

"What happens on the road, stays on the road."

55

"Don't care. If that's what you need to get your rocks off, go elsewhere. I'm not interested." He took another long draw on his smoke, before blowing it out.

"Dude, I don't need shit to get my rocks off. All I'm saying is if you need a little light relief, let me know. None of the boys would say anything. A break is a break."

He nodded.

"Hey, Lucius, introduce me to your son," one of the women with long green hair said, taking a seat by Lucius.

"Sinner, this is Roxy. She's one of the best fucks you can imagine."

Roxy rolled her eyes. "Hey, sunshine. I have wanderlust every summer and fall. I call Lucius here, meet up with him, and we have a good couple of months together before I go back home."

"I thought you were on the road all the time."

Roxy shook her head. "A girl can live on the road without the simple pleasures for a short time, but I like what I like."

"She misses my dick," Lucius said.

Sinner saw the two were just good friends. Relaxing back, Sinner simply basked in the enjoyment of having no worries, no stress, and just fun.

They stayed at the little pit stop for two hours. During that time, he was introduced to some of his fellow buddies. They mocked his leather jacket and the stitching of his patch.

Ignoring them, he took it all in good fun. By the time he was ready to get on the road, he was itching to have the machine beneath him.

There was something about working his way around the roads that thrilled him to the core.

Time passed, and he watched as a couple of the

guys goofed around, overtaking each other on the roads. By nightfall, there was no motel in sight, so they set up a small camp off the main road. The women gathered up bits of wood while the men set about building a fire, and putting down some blankets that they kept.

"It's all about being prepared," Lucius said. "I reckon two hours riding tomorrow, we'll find a diner. There's always one around."

Sinner glanced past Lucius's shoulder, and saw Roxy sitting on the ground. She had a bottle of water, and was downing some pills.

"What's the deal with Roxy?" Sinner asked.

"I thought you didn't want to fuck around?"

"I don't. She's ... different."

Lucius sighed and glanced over at Roxy, who was leaning against a large boulder. She looked tired. "She may be dying."

"What?" Sinner asked.

"She has the shittiest kind of luck in the world. When she was a kid, she got cancer, and she beat it. Every year without fail she goes home, takes her tests, lives her little life. Her childhood was spent in sterile rooms, and being looked at, poked every which way they could to fight it. When she was free, she broke free."

"She's got cancer again?" Sinner asked.

"That may be the case. They found a lump in her breast. She is waiting to hear about the results, and while she waits, she is going to spend the time partying it up."

"You care about her?"

"Of course, I do. She's my best friend. The only friend I've really got. The real kind of friend." He shook his head, and Sinner saw the emotion in the guy's face. "There's a reason I don't settle down, Sinner. Once you settle down, you allow yourself to feel, and some of us, we've had enough agony to last me a lifetime." Lucius looked back at Roxy. "She could be sick, and this could be her last year riding. I'm not going to force her to go home and rest. I'm going to give her what she wants."

"You don't know if that's what she is fighting?"

Lucius shrugged. "Live in the moment, Sinner. You never know when it may be your last."

Later that night, Sinner sat a few feet away from the rest of the crew. He had a beer in one hand. One of the guys had actually thought to bring the alcohol. It didn't matter to him. It was warm, but it was wet. Staring up at the stars, Sinner wondered if Lola had forgotten about him. He smiled, recalling how distracted she used to get.

He was about to give up when his cell phone lit up with her name.

"Hello," he said.

"Sinner, I am so sorry. Lacey and her girls didn't leave until late. I am so sorry."

"You don't have to worry. Did you have a good day?"

"Yeah, I did. Lacey wanted to dye my hair again, but I've said I'm going to let the color grow out, and you know, just be me once again."

He remembered her golden brown locks.

"Sounds good to me. I met up with a few friends, and they're partying."

"Did you find yourself a motel?"

"Nope. It's just me, you, and the stars."

"And your friends in the distance? Should I be worried about your safety?"

"They're allies, babe. You don't have to worry about me."

"I thought I may have to call someone to come and find you," she said.

"I can take care of myself. So, what are you

wearing?" He heard some rustling.

"Nothing now, and I'm in bed."

"You're all alone."

"Of course. Lacey's headed back home, and it's just me alone in my apartment, and now I'm talking with you."

His cock thickened. Maybe it was in his head, but he was sure he heard a sultry moan from her.

"Completely naked?" he asked. "No panties, no pajamas?" She used to love teasing him with all the different negligees she used to wear.

"Completely naked. No clothes on at all, Oh, I lie, the blanket is over me."

He let out a groan. "Tell me if you want this to stop?" he asked.

"Oh, why, Sinner? What do you want me to do?"

"I want you to touch your pussy for me."

His cock was pressing against his zipper. Putting his beer on the ground beside him, he down eased the zipper of his jeans and took his cock out. The tip was already coated in pre-cum.

She gasped, and he groaned. Closing his eyes, he could see her as clear as if he was there, the way she would be spread out before him.

"I'm wet for you, Sinner. So wet for you."

"Is your pussy nice and swollen for me, wanting my cock?"

"Yes. I want you, Sinner."

"Put a finger inside you. Press it in deep." The moment she did, the moan across the line got a little deeper. Her pussy was always so tight. She fit his cock like a vise, and right now, he wanted to do nothing more than sink inside her.

Instead, he wrapped his fingers around his length, and started to work up and down the tip.

"What are you doing?" she asked.

"I've got my cock in my hand. The tip is already wet for you."

"I love your cock. It's always so big."

It had taken him months to get her to say the word "cock". Hearing it from her voice right now was a victory.

This time apart is working.

She's finding herself.

From the moment he had met Lola, after everything the Master had done to her, she'd been withdrawn, and she had always just done what was asked of her. She never did what she wanted. It was one of the reasons he'd found it hard not to let her go when she wanted to. This was something *she* wanted to do. The apartment, her job, her friends, this was all something she had been able to do without asking him. For that, he was so damn happy.

Joy filled him.

"If you were here right now with me, what would you do?" he asked. "My big cock is waiting for you."

"I'd sink to my knees, Sinner. I'd want to taste your cock. Is it as nice as I remember?"

"Nothing has changed about me, baby. Believe me. I'd give you my cock, let it hit the back of that pretty throat."

She whimpered.

"You'd love that, wouldn't you, baby? You'd love to have my cock filling your mouth, and then have me bending you over the bed, and filling your sweet cunt."

"Oh, Sinner. I want you. I want your tongue, your fingers."

"Come for me, Lola. Scream my name."

"Sinner!" She yelled his name, and he groaned,

calling out hers as he spilled his seed onto his naked stomach. He was pleased that he'd had the foresight to remove his shirt.

They were both gasping for breath, and panting.

"I love you, Sinner."

"I love you, too, baby."

He rested against the boulder, closing his eyes, as she enjoyed the post-bliss of his orgasm.

"I can't move," she said, giggling.

"Neither can I. I don't want to move."

Silence fell between them, but for the first time it wasn't uncomfortable. It was something else.

"I want to do this with you, Sinner."

"Phone sex?"

"I want us to talk, to share messages, and pictures. I want to see your life, and I want to share mine with you."

"Long-distance relationship?"

"Lacey told me that she can see a difference in me. Can you? I don't want to give up on us."

"I don't want to give up on us either. My love for you has always been there, babe. I get it now. Being on the road, I get what you want, and what you need. I'm with you every step of the way."

"So, sharing stuff with each other? You're open to that?"

"Yeah, I am. More than you can know. So, I've got a little task for you," he said.

"I'm all ears."

He chuckled. "I want you to go into a sex shop, and purchase a dildo of your choice."

"Saucy."

"I want you to do that by tomorrow."

"It's Sunday tomorrow."

"Some places are open. I'd like to see how far we

can do this."

"Sinner, you're a wicked man," she said.

"Don't you forget it either."

He heard her sigh.

"I love you."

"I love you, too, baby. I'm going to let you go. Do your research, and let me know when you find it." He hung up the phone, grabbed his beer, and took a long swallow.

"You really do love her, don't you?" Roxy asked.

He opened his eyes, and saw Roxy leaning on the boulder staring down at him. "You may want to clean that up as well. Dried cum is the worst."

He laughed, and cleaned away his orgasm with a shirt he was going to have to toss out. "I need to stop for clothes."

"I'll let Lucius know."

"How long were you sitting there?" he asked.

"I was leaning over the rock for the past couple of minutes. It sounded important, and I think the best thing is not come between a man and his orgasm."

He put his cock away and finished his beer. Roxy took a seat beside him.

"This is not creepy at all," he said.

"Ha-ha." Roxy handed him another beer. "The guys are good for something, and making sure they have beer is one of them." She clinked her bottle to his. "You didn't answer my question."

"Yeah, I love her. She's my soul."

"That's very romantic."

"Should you be drinking?" he asked. "I saw you taking some pills earlier."

"Don't be a party pooper. There's a lot of things I shouldn't have done. I'm still doing them." She rested her head back against the boulder. "I'm dying."

He paused, and looked at her.

"What?"

"Does that surprise you?" she asked.

He stared down at his beer.

"How old are you?"

"I'm twenty-five years old, and according to the doctors, I won't see my next birthday."

He didn't know what to say.

"I've surprised you, haven't I?"

"Just a bit."

"God, I always wanted so much. I've not told Lucius, not yet. He doesn't need to know."

"Roxy—"

"Don't say anything to him yet. I can't bring myself to tell him. Cancer is a son of a bitch, isn't it?"

He saw there were tears in her eyes.

"I wanted so much. Kids, a family, a life. Some of us really do get the shitty stuff in life, don't we?"

"Why are you telling me this?" he asked. "You don't know me."

"You won't tell anyone, not even Lucius. I needed to tell someone, and you're a newbie."

"What about the other women?" Couldn't she have picked anyone but him?

She shook her head. "We're not close friends. We share one love, and that is the love of partying. I've got nothing else to share with them." She stared up at the stars. "I take the pills because it helps to take the pain away. I could be in a hospital, hooked up to tubes, puking my guts up, and wishing for it to end, and I could spend my last days doing that. I wanted to be on the road, riding on the back of Lucius's bike."

"You need to tell him."

"When I'm ready."

"If you didn't want him to know, why tell me?

You don't strike me as a woman who'll open up to total strangers."

"You're a good guy. You will know what to do when the time is right. Lucius doesn't love me like you love your woman. He cares about me a lot, but I think when I go, it will hit him hard. If you're still around, will you keep an eye on him? Help him?"

He stared at her, really looked at her, and it was then that he saw how ill she was. "How long are we talking?"

"A couple of months. I may not even last that long." Tears glistened in her eyes. "Life really is shitty."

"Roxy."

"Don't. Please. Don't change or be different with me. I couldn't stand that." She rested her head on his shoulder.

What the fuck had just happened?

Chapter Six

Piston County

"Dad, what's a pussy?"

Devil paused on his bike and looked over to his son. A son that was growing up too fast and scaring him with each passing day. It was Sunday morning, and while Lexie was working on dinner, he was working on his bike. They were having Ripper and Judi over, along with their kids. Natalie had also been invited over, which would bring Butler and Slash. His house was turning into a fucking love next.

"Why do you want to know?" he asked.

"What is it?"

"It's another word to call a cat," he said. *Ha, easy way out of that one.*

"Why does Slash want to lick a cat?"

The wrench Devil was holding clattered to the ground, and he glanced up at his son. "Excuse me?"

"Can you lick cats? That's gross. They lick themselves all the time."

"Please tell me what you heard? Did Slash know you were there?"

Simon shook his head. "Nope. He didn't. He was staring in the mirror, and he was repeating words."

"Like what."

"'Natalie, why don't we go and have some fun? Natalie, I want to lick your pussy,'" Simon deepened his voice, and Devil hung his head.

"How about we have this talk when you know what reproduction is?"

"Tell me what it is?" Simon asked.

"Son, do you want to have an hour on my cell phone to talk to Tabby?" he asked.

"Yes, yes. What do I have to do?"

"Not talk about pussy, or ask any questions about reproduction until you're … fifteen?" Devil asked.

"Awesome. Total deal, Dad." Simon ran over, shook his hand, and Devil couldn't believe he was bribing chat time with his son.

Maybe Tabby wouldn't be such a bad idea as a daughter-in-law.

"You're just too funny," Lexie said, drawing his attention behind him.

"You heard that?"

"Maybe I should warn Eva that you're using her daughter to get out of tricky situations."

"I'm going to kill Slash. I really am."

"Come on, it's cute. He's like a teenage boy with his first crush."

"He's a thirty-year-old man, and he doesn't need to practice asking a girl out."

"Natalie is not like every other woman. You have to admit, practice is needed with her."

"He has to be careful. Simon's getting more curious every single day. I don't want to get a call from social fucking services because he's repeated what some of the guys have said."

"We'll handle everything, Devil. You worry way too much." She wrapped her arms around, and he hugged her tight.

"You always make me feel better about shit."

He saw the flash of sadness in her eyes, and he knew why. "Don't talk about her, babe. *You're* his mother. No one else."

She sighed. "Kayla—"

"No, Lexie. We agreed. She gave him up to you, and even though she was killed … I'm not going to confuse him."

"You know Simon hears stuff he's not meant to. What are we going to do if he hears one too many things? Are you just going to constantly keep him in the dark?" Lexie asked.

He stroked her cheek. He loved this woman more than anything. She had stripped just to take care of Simon. Simon was not her son, and he was, in fact, her nephew. She was not his mother, and Devil hated that. It was his biggest mistake, even though he loved his son so much. He wished with all of his fucking heart, which was owned by Lexie, that Simon was hers. "You're too good for me, Lexie."

The moment he had seen her, Devil had known without a doubt that he was going to love her, forever, and for always.

"I love you, too, Devil. You know that is not going to change, even if you try to distract me."

"You know me so well."

"I know you better than you know yourself." She pressed a kiss to his lips. "Think about it." She pulled away, and he watched her walk in.

"Did I miss the fun?" Slash asked.

Devil turned toward the man that had pissed him off. "Next time you preen or try to figure out how to get in Natalie's pussy, do it in the privacy of your bedroom, or far away from ears."

Slash frowned. "What?"

"Simon heard you. I don't want to talk about trying to explain why you want to lick a pussy to my son. He thinks you like cats, Slash." Devil watched as Slash paled. "Just so you know, women don't want to hear you talking about licking their pussy until you get past the first date."

"This is embarrassing."

"You like Natalie?"

"Yeah, I do."

"Then figure out a way to tell her. She's a smart woman. Ask, and she may surprise you." Devil held his hands out. "You know what, I'm done. I don't know when I became the advice giver, but I'm done."

"Wait, Devil."

When had he become the man they all turned to for relationship advice?" *Duh, you're married with five kids. You're a success.*

Turning back to Slash, he smiled. "Yes."

"What about Butler? I think he likes her as well."

"The thing about Butler, he likes people who are not complicated. Natalie is a pure soul. She doesn't challenge his other needs. He finds peace with her. Advice is now done." He held his hands up, and left.

****

"These are awesome," Butler said.

Natalie smiled, tucking some hair behind her ear. They were her latest clothing sketches. She had been working on different fabrics and was hoping to have some new ideas for the next year. Working for Lexie with their clothing shop was a dream come true. She didn't have to give up her dream. The problem was the ranch.

Her family was dead, and all that remained was herself. The ranch was hard work, and there were days that she woke up hating life.

"Thanks."

They were not her best work. She knew it.

Taking the folder from him, she watched the children in Lexie and Devil's backyard. She loved coming here. The love was so clear to see, and she loved being part of it.

"Something is bothering you. What is it?"

"It's nothing. Not really. I'm just—"

"Don't lie to me. That's what you have Slash for."

She held onto her art book, and for a split second, she hated Butler. He always saw through her.

"You're a pain. You know that, right?"

He rolled his eyes. "You're not the first person to tell me that. You won't be the last. Just a word of warning. I've learned how to be a hard ass. It's part of my charm. Talk to me."

"I want to move away from the ranch. I know my dad sold it to Devil, and you guys have been helping me out, but I can't do this anymore." She refused to cry. She had cried enough and wouldn't be doing it again any time soon. "You could have kicked me out long ago."

"That's not what we wanted, Natalie."

"Tomorrow, I'm going to go to Devil. He can do what he wants with the land. Sell it off, use it. I don't care. I want out."

"You're sure."

"Today I woke up, and if I hadn't thought about coming here, I didn't want to wake up. I didn't want to deal with life. I don't like waking up, and wishing I wasn't here, Butler."

"What does Slash say?"

"He tells me to keep my chin up. That my worries are not there, and that I can do anything. I believe him, but … ranching was never my dream. I like creating stuff. I've not been able to finish a single project in months."

"You don't need to rush," Butler said.

"The point is, *this* is what I want to do. I'm not leaving, or going anywhere else. I want to create, and have new lines every year for Lexie, and the store. The online market is flourishing. We have a huge market right now, and I don't want to lose that."

Butler took her hand, and she saw the scars on the back of his. He was such a good friend. "I'm here, Natalie. Do what you want, and I will help you anyway that I can."

She smiled. "Thank you, Butler."

"Hey, Natalie," Slash said.

Turning her smile to Slash, she saw him glance down at Butler's hand.

She didn't want to let Butler go, and she gripped his hand even tighter.

****

Lola logged onto her computer and put a search in for the local sex shop. When she found one that was open, she couldn't stop smiling. It was the strangest feeling in the world. Bag in hand, she ventured out on a Sunday morning, which was strange for her. She usually preferred staying in and being a slob watching television.

Leaving her apartment into the crisp air was a welcome relief. She felt invigorated. Last night felt like a step in the right direction.

The walk to the sex shop only took twenty minutes, and she was a little embarrassed to go inside. She went for a coffee, and played around with her phone for a little bit.

Lola: **Do I need to go?**

Sinner: **Sex shop?**

Lola: **Yeah.**

Sinner: **Do you want to have some fun tonight?**

She giggled. Glancing around, she waited to see if someone was watching her. No one was interested.

Lola: **Give me a little taste of what is to come?**

Sinner: **... No. trust me.**

Lola: **hate you.**

Sinner: **tonight you won't be.**

Pocketing her cell phone, she finished her coffee,

paid the bill, and finally filled with courage to finally go into the sex shop.

The door closed, and she didn't even realize that she had closed her eyes.

"Are you okay?"

She opened her eyes to see a woman there. She was young, perhaps in college.

"Hey," she said, her cheeks heating as she moved away from the door.

"You're a virgin."

"Excuse me?"

"You're a virgin to the world of sex shops. It's okay. Nothing here will bite unless you want it to," the woman said. "Have a look around, and if you need anything, don't be afraid to shout."

Lola nodded, and holding her bag close to her, she started to look at the many array of different devices.

What the hell?

Lola was completely out of her depth. When she saw some rings that were labelled cock rings, she couldn't resist. Snapping them on her cell phone, she sent the picture to Sinner asking if he'd like them as a present.

She had a second to wait before he replied.

Sinner: **Very funny.**

It was like she could hear his laughter, and it calmed her. There was whips and chains. She posed, took a quick snap, and sent it to him.

Her first picture for him in months. Her heart was racing as she waited.

Sinner: **You're beautiful. Get a crop if you want it used on your ass.**

She moved away from the crops. There was no way anything like that was being used on her skin.

Through the shop, she went around, snapping random pictures, and as she did, she forgot about the woman in the shop, or the other customers that had filtered through. When her cell phone began to ring, she jumped.

Sinner was calling.

"Hey, honey," she said, answering.

"Are you still in the shop?"

"Of course. I'm still trying to decide. It's hard to do." She hummed. "Should I get a vibrator, nipple clamps? This is like a treasure trove of pleasure. Why have I not been here before?"

Sinner growled. "If I was there right now, I'd be doing nothing but naughty things to you."

"I wish you were here." She licked her lips and told him her address. "I just thought you'd like to know in case you were ever close to me, you know?"

"I've already got your address, babe. Lexie gave it to me, and now that I know I'm invited, I'll certainly think about it."

She smiled. "So, what do you think? Vibrator, dildo."

"Get all three."

"Three?"

"Get the nipple clamps. When you're confident enough you could send me a picture. I would love to see you in them."

She grew wet thinking of taking pictures of herself for him to see.

"Can I ask you something?" he said.

"Of course."

"If you know someone was sick, and they were keeping that sickness to themselves, what would you do?"

"Wow, talk about a biggie. I don't know. Are you sick?"

"No. A friend of a friend. She told me but won't

let me tell another friend."

"It's a she?" She couldn't help the strike of jealousy that rushed through her. *Your fault. You could be at Piston County without any of this.*

"Yeah. I met her yesterday. She's sick, and I know her friend. Anyway, it's complicated. Forget I asked."

Feeling like the worst girlfriend in the world, if that was even what she was anymore, she offered her advice. "There's a reason she told *you*, and not her friend. It's not your secret, Sinner. Would you want someone to tell that secret if it was you?"

"No. You're right." There was some commotion, and she knew what he was going to say next. "I've got to go. Chat soon, babe."

He was gone, and she stared at her phone once again. "Have a nice day, Sinner."

What did you expect? Huh, you left Piston County on this bright idea of finding yourself, of being whole. What is whole? Is it being able to go to a sex shop without fear?

Forcing her head back to the now, she picked up the vibrator, the dildo, and nipple clamps.

She purchased them, and was still able to smile at the woman serving her. Points for not completely losing it. She felt better at least.

Taking her prizes back to her apartment, she sat down on her sofa with them on the table in front of her. Any arousal she had was completely gone.

This wasn't about Sinner's predicament with the other woman either. No, this was about her own problems. Master. The guy who had taken her. He'd ordered her to call him Master, but the truth was, his name was Andrew.

He was dead.

There was no danger of him ever coming back.

Rubbing at her temples, she tried to clear her head.

Sitting alone in her apartment wasn't helping her. Without grabbing anything, she left her comfortable place on the sofa, to go for a walk. She didn't watch where she was going, or even take stock of what she was doing. She just kept on going.

"Lola, please talk to us."

"Mom, I've got nothing to talk about."

"You've got to talk to someone about what happened. You won't go near a computer, and you won't even help in the kitchen. We're worried about you, honey, and we're allowed to be worried."

"You don't need to be worried about me. I'm fine."

She hadn't stayed with her parents for that long after her recovery. Every second she had stayed with them, she couldn't help but wonder what they were thinking. She would catch her father staring at her, the pity in his eyes, making her sick to her stomach. It had been the final straw for her, which was why she ended up going to Piston County.

She found a bench in the center of the city, and she took a seat. Even for a Sunday it was busy, and she watched people, wondering not for the first time what they were all thinking or feeling. Did they even care what was going on in everyone's life? Or maybe they had their own troubles and it didn't matter.

There was a couple coming out of a clothing store. They looked wealthy, and she watched as the guy held the woman. He cupped her cheek and tilted her head back. It was as if everyone else faded as they looked at each other.

There was a mother with a child, and they were

rushing past.

A guy walked past on his cell phone. "Yeah, yeah, I've told her I'm working late. When can I see you?"

She didn't even know what that was about. On and on life passed her by, and she stayed still on the bench, wondering what she was going to do with *her* life. Time passed, and it was only when she noticed that it was dark, that she had a start.

Getting to her feet, she made her way back to her apartment, and before she could stop herself, she dialed Whizz's number.

"Does it ever end?" Lola asked, trying to contain her sobs. "Does this feeling of being completely disconnected ever stop? Is there a way back, or do you just put on a good show?"

"Lola."

"No, please don't pity me. I don't want pity. I want the truth."

"It … gets better. That's all I can really say. I'm not waiting for bad shit to happen anymore. You don't have to keep looking for him, Lola. You're free."

"I don't feel free. I feel trapped, and I hate it. He's a monster, Whizz, and he's dead."

"I know."

"He's dead. Why did he do this to me? Why am I still letting him do this to me? I had a good thing. I had a great thing, and I'm here, and Sinner's somewhere else. Why?" She couldn't stop the screaming and the crying.

"You did what you had to do. You're strong, Lola. You can do this. I promise you."

Over and over, Whizz kept talking to her as she collapsed on her apartment floor and sobbed out every part of her pain that she could. There was nothing else she could do.

Chapter Seven

"Hey, baby," Sinner said. He had caved and asked Devil to pay for the hotel room.

"Hey," Lola said.

The moment she spoke, he knew something was wrong.

"What is it? What's wrong?" he asked.

She didn't make a sound for so long that he was worried he had missed something. "Lola?"

"I'm fine, Sinner. I have a headache. It has been a long day."

"Did you have time to play with your new toys?"

"I'm not going to be up for anything like that tonight."

Sinner sat down on the bed, and waited. "Talk to me, Lola."

"Have I ruined us, Sinner? Is there any hope for us for the future?"

"Of course."

"No bullshit?"

"That's not bullshit, babe. That's the truth. You're still my girl, right?"

"Am I?" she asked. "I left."

"Let's get past that. You're my girl, Lola. Tell me who do you belong to?" he asked.

"You. I'll always belong to you."

Sinner sat back, and his heart was pounding. Was she about to open up to him? They hadn't talked about her time being kidnapped, trapped, beaten. He knew everything, and he had never pushed. What he'd done was try to protect her every chance he got. He had fucked up the most when it came to her.

"He's always there inside my head. I can't make

him stop, and it's killing me."

He closed his eyes, and even as he felt relief, he knew this was his chance, and he couldn't fuck that up.

"I don't know what to do. Look at what I've already done. I've left a life I love. I love you, Sinner, and I love our life in Piston County. What am I doing?"

She was growing. She was healing.

"You're doing what you need to do, Lola. I'm proud of you."

Lola growled. "I … I need to be better for you, Sinner. I had to be the woman you deserved. I don't want you freaking out about a cage, or something else that could trigger bad memories. He was violent, vicious, and cruel. You are not any of those things, and I always knew that."

Again, he didn't say anything, waiting for her to speak.

"I was walking home when I was taken. It was painful, and the pain didn't stop for a long time. If I didn't do what he said fast enough, he'd hurt me."

"I wish I could take that pain away from you, baby. You know I'd do that for you in a heartbeat."

"I know. You've always been so good for me, even when I've not deserved it." She cried. "I didn't think I'd ever get out, and I begged for death. After everything that happened. What makes it worse, Paris was with me. I saw what they did to her, and part of me was glad." She stopped, and he heard the pain inside her. He had known this all along. Even Paris had known it. "I was pleased that they had picked her and not me. I hated knowing what I did. How could Paris be friends with me when I was glad that they hurt her and not me? I'm such a horrible person."

Sinner felt completely helpless, and he forced the tears back. She didn't need him weak, even though when it came to his woman, he completely was.

"Paris felt the same way."

"She would distract them when she could," Lola said. "She would try and save me, and I didn't say anything." Another pause. "I'm so ashamed. I don't deserve her forgiveness or her friendship. I'm a horrible person."

Sinner didn't even think. He checked the time, and knew that if he rode all night, he would be with her by morning.

"It's not your fault. What happened had nothing to do with you, babe."

"I have to go now, Sinner. I need to … I don't know…"

The line went dead.

"Lola? Lola? Fuck." He left his apartment and went to Lucius's door and knocked. "I've got to head out. My woman needs me."

"Go. We'll meet up soon."

He nodded. Without looking back, he went to his bike, straddled his machine, and headed toward his woman. Sinner didn't know if this was the start of their relationship again. He only knew that he had to hug her, to be with her, and make sure she was okay.

****

Lola couldn't sleep. She drank her wine as she looked through the pictures that she had taken home with her. When she finished her first bottle of wine, she grabbed the second bottle. The hours ticked by, and as they did, she became even more guilty as memories of their time unfolded in her mind once again.

Each punishment. Each pain.

What kind of friend was she if she was happy to see Paris was taken and not her? She had been young, weak, and pathetic. She hated herself, and that was another reason she had to get out of Piston County.

Paris deserved a better friend than she was.

Around four in the morning, she crashed out from the drink and exhaustion. She was on her sitting room floor, curled up in a ball surrounded by all of her pictures. The memories she had tried to fight, to hide from.

At seven o'clock a knock at the door woke her up. She rolled over and frowned as she heard Sinner's voice. It was impossible. There was no way that it could be his voice. He was nowhere near her.

"Lola, baby, open up. I need to know that you're okay." He hit her door, and she rolled over, even as her head began to pound. The events and the truths she'd told the night before came back to haunt her, pushing everything back into clarity.

Getting to her feet was hard. Her head was throbbing, and her stomach wanted to empty its contents. She ignored it all and went to her door.

She removed each chain with a shaking hand. She wasn't nervous, not even slightly. Licking her parched lips, she opened her door, and there he was, Sinner.

"Sinner," she said his name, afraid that he would disappear.

In one step, she was in his arms. Within a second, his lips were on hers, and she felt safe. She felt like everything she had faced had been worth it.

Lola knew she was nowhere near to being healed. She was just starting.

"What happened wasn't your fault," he said.

"I'm a monster, Sinner. I disgust myself."

"No." He cupped her face, and forced her to look at him. "Look at me, Lola." When she didn't, he gave her a rough shake. "Look at me." She opened her eyes, and stared at him. The love in them shone back. "You were taken against your will. You were picked because of your skill. He didn't give a shit about how to keep you in line, so he used fear. You were young, a girl, and he tore every innocent thing away from you."

"How can you even look at me after everything I've felt?" she asked. "Who wants someone who is happy that another was hurting?"

"Did you want Paris to be hurt? Even if there was no risk to you?"

"No, of course not. I would never want Paris hurt. She is my friend, and I love her."

"That's what makes you a good person. The choice was taken out of your hands. You and Paris didn't have a single choice in what happened to you," he said. He stroked her face. "What you went through, to me, you are one of the bravest women I've ever known. I'm proud of what you've been able to accomplish. You couldn't even touch a computer for the longest time. I love you, Lola. Even after what we've been through. You leaving me, I didn't get it in the beginning, but now, I see it, and I see you." He stared at her in a way that he'd never done before.

It was like his eyes were open clearly, and he finally saw the real her, the person she'd been trying to be.

"This is not who I was meant to be," she said.

"You're exactly how you should be, babe. No one, and I mean no one, can take anything away from you. You've earned everything in life. That shit with Andrew, it meant nothing, it is nothing. You do not need to think about it. You do not need to be guilty for your feelings. That was another time, and you cannot allow it to bring you down." He pressed his lips against her forehead, and Lola closed her eyes, basking in his touch. "You have come a long way," he said.

"What do you mean?"

"You wouldn't have opened up to me like this."

"I told you everything," she said, pulling away a little but not so far that his hands wouldn't be on her.

"No, you didn't. You rarely talked about how you were thinking or feeling. I always had to guess. It was nearly impossible to reach you, babe. You just didn't want to talk to me. I didn't know what to do."

She stared at him, thinking it couldn't be true, and yet, that was exactly what it was, true. When she woke up at night, she would just have him hold her, and she'd tell him that Master or Andrew had visited her dreams. Depending on how scary it was, depended on who visited. They were both the same person, but she had known Master first. That had been his name, the person she had no choice but to follow. Andrew was the name she had learned a little later, the name he went by in the world, and it tormented her at times that she had two sides to one hell.

Sinner ran his hands up and down her arms, and she felt like crap, the worst kind of crap.

"This is good for you," he said. "Being away from the club. Setting up your new life. I didn't think it was, and I didn't know why you were doing it, but I know now, and all I can say is sorry, babe. Sorry for being a complete and total asshole to you when you really didn't deserve it." He leaned in close, and put another kiss to her head. "I love you, Lola, more than anything."

She held onto his arms, knowing and feeling that love deep in her core. They were not just empty words, but there was real emotion and feeling behind it.

"I once heard someone say something, and it went along the lines, that if you loved someone, truly loved them, you'd let them go. I didn't think for a second that it was possible to let anyone go. You help them, and you guide them. But now I see that if you really want someone to thrive, to be better, to find themselves, then you have to learn to let them go. Not in the way that we'll never see each other, but knowing in my head and heart, that somehow, we will find our way back to each other."

She grabbed his jacket and pulled him close. Wrapping her arms around his neck, she pressed her lips against his.

This was not the start of their new beginning. She had to finish this. She had to finish what she had started, but no matter what, her mind, her body, her heart, and her very soul belonged to him. Nothing was going to change that.

"Make love to me, Sinner."

She didn't need to ask him twice. He picked her up and carried her through to the bedroom that she pointed out. He placed her on the bed, and she watched as he removed his jacket.

Her pussy grew slick as he tugged off his shirt, and then she realized that she was just gawking at him. Tearing at her own clothes, she matched him in speed as she removed hers. The moment they were both naked, she threw herself at him.

He caught her around the waist, and together they fell to the bed. She moaned as his hard cock pressed against her stomach.

Reaching down, she wrapped her fingers around the length, and started to work from his balls up to the tip, and down again. Pre-cum already leaking out of the little slit at the top.

Sinner groaned and caught her hand, pressing them either side of her head. "It has been too long for me."

"Too long?"

"Yes. There are no women for me on the roads. All I have is our memories that we created."

She loved this man, more than anything, she loved him. He released her hands and kissed her lips, trailing them down to her breasts. He flicked the tips of each of her breasts, and she arched up, aching, and needing him.

"Who do you belong to?"

"You, Sinner, just you. There's no one else."

"Damn right, there's no one else. Only I will ever know the taste of your pussy. Only I will know how hard your nipples get when they went to be sucked. You want my cock, don't you, babe? You want it so deep inside you, that you can forget about everything else."

"Yes!" She screamed the word, unable to hold back. It had been too long since she had been with him, and now that he was here in the flesh, she had to have him. To love him, to fuck him.

Sinner kissed down her belly, making her giggle as he stopped at her stomach, and gave a little growl and nibble. He didn't linger for long, and trailed his lips between her thighs.

She opened her legs.

"Show me this pretty pussy," he said.

She held the lips of her sex open, showing him what he wanted. When his tongue touched, she gasped at the sensation. He swirled around her clit, and moved down, going to her entrance. The sensation was … amazing.

He plundered inside her, and then brought his tongue up to tease her clit.

"You're so wet and juicy, Lola. I could lick you all day long, and I've got time."

"I'm all yours, Sinner. Every single part of me

belongs to you. Forever and always." Whatever path they were taking, and she didn't completely understand it, but it was happening, she just knew they were going to find their way together again.

He gripped her hips, spreading open her thighs until she was arching up into his touch. "So fucking perfect," he said, growling the words against her flesh. She loved it when he did that, and when he tugged her clit into his mouth, using his teeth to create just enough pain that it has her gasping and begging for more.

"You know what I want," he said.

Sinner wanted her complete surrender, and she gave it. She gave herself to him, riding up against his face, needing him more than she had ever needed anything else.

"Come all over my face, baby. I want to taste all of you, every single part."

Gripping the sheets beneath her, she screamed his name as he focused on her clit, sliding his tongue back and forth, building up a release that was so earth-shattering, she didn't think she would ever have the strength for more.

Before her orgasm was even over, Sinner was between her thighs and inside her. He filled her to the brim, and she stared right into his eyes as he claimed her, loving every part of him.

"This, right here, this feeling of being inside you, that's what I'm fighting for, and that's what I know we're going to keep on having." He pulled out of her until only the very tip of him was within her, then slammed every inch inside her. "Am I hurting you?"

"No. You're not hurting me. I love it. Please, don't stop."

He grabbed hold of her hands, and like many times before, he pinned her to the bed, only this time, there was no initial fear, nor need to get away. She thrust up to meet his cock, begging for more, and knowing in her heart and in her head, that she had finally found what she was looking for.

Chapter Eight

"Would you like to see what I got from that sex shop?" Lola asked.

Sinner stroked his finger down her arm, and smiled. "I couldn't believe it when you posed those pictures."

"Believe it, buster. Would you like to see?"

"Yeah, I would." Sinner eased back, and expected her to cover up, getting dressed before she ventured out of her room. She didn't. She rushed into the sitting room, her ass bare for him to see and admire as she walked away from him, all of her glorious curves on display for him, making his mouth water.

"Here we go," she said, coming into the room, and holding a dildo and a vibrator. "What do you think?"

He held each one up and was impressed. "I'm still in shock you went to a sex shop."

"On my own as well." She tucked some hair behind her ears. "I'm sorry about my crazed meltdown."

"It was long overdue. I was hoping you'd cave a few years ago," he said. "This is a little small compared to me, don't you think?"

"I didn't get it to replace you. You asked for me to get it."

"And I think before we go, I should have a little play." He moved, picking her up, and tossing her to the bed so that she once again landed on her back.

"You're going back on the road?" she asked.

He nodded. "Yeah, there's something that I need to do first." He needed to be with Roxy and with Lucius. There were no words that would make any sense, but it was something that he had to do."

"I get it. I do."

"You don't, but one day I will tell you all about it." Removing the protective packaging from the dildo, he climbed off the bed, ordering her to stay in the same place. Giving the dildo a wash, he returned to find her playing with her pussy, two fingers running between her slit, which was driving him crazy. "Look at you, naughty girl."

She smiled. "You love it."

He really did. Climbing on the bed, he placed the dildo on the covers, and then grabbed her hips, moving her so that she was on her knees. She groaned but moved into the position that he wanted.

"I want you to grab your ass, and spread those cheeks wide. Show me that ass and pussy."

Lola did exactly as he asked, and he groaned, wanting both. He wanted inside her pussy again, but he also wanted to claim her ass. Sliding his thumb inside her pussy, he coated it with her cream and drew it back to her puckered hole. She let out a little whimper, and he smiled. Stroking her anus, he watched her response, and with his other hand, he stroked her clit.

"Do you like that, baby?" he asked.

"Yes."

"Do you want me to stop?"

"No!" She yelled that word.

"Beg me."

"Please, don't stop. I want it, Sinner. I want you."

He pressed against her ass and removed his fingers from her pussy at the same time. Picking up the dildo, he rubbed it against her wet slit, coating it. When he was sure it was nice and slick, he began to ease it inside her.

With his thumb, he pressed it past that tight ring of muscles, and began to pump inside her.

"Oh, fuck!"

He paused, making sure she was okay, and only when he was certain that she was fine did he begin again.

Thrusting the dildo inside her, he pulled his thumb from her ass, and used a finger instead, and started to stretch her.

"Do you like this, babe? Do you like having my fingers inside your pretty ass?"

"Yes."

"It looks so pretty, opening up to me." The thrusts with the dildo increased, and he worked a second finger into her ass, spreading her open. In and out, he worked her ass and her pussy. All the time, his cock got a little bigger, getting harder with each second that he was watching.

Lola was submitting to him in ways that she had never done before. There was still a barrier, something holding them apart, but together they were going to work through it. At least while they were apart they were going to do it.

She belonged to him, and she owned him. There was no other word for it. There was no one else in the world for him but her. He loved her more than anything, and would do whatever it took to make her feel safe.

When her ass took his fingers without any restraint, he eased the dildo out of her ass, and pressed it against the slight opening of her ass. Slowly, he eased his fingers out of her anus, and pushed the dildo, inch by inch, inside her. The fake cock was a lot bigger than his fingers, and she moaned, pushing back against the dick.

He pushed the cock inside her ass until she had taken it all.

Grabbing his own cock, he placed the tip at her entrance, and began to sink inside her sweet pussy, and it was nice and tight. When all of him was inside her to the fucking hilt, he grabbed her hips, and basked in the feel of her tight cunt squeezing him.

Closing his eyes, he relished every second of pleasure until she began to wriggle on his cock. He couldn't hold on any longer, so with aching tenderness, he started to slowly make love to her.

"Do you feel full, babe?" he asked. A cock was in her pussy, and one in her ass.

"Yes."

"Do you want me to stop?"

"No," she said with a little growl, which he found to be so adorable and so damn sexy. He wouldn't ever get tired of fucking her, of needing her. "Please don't stop, Sinner. I don't want you to stop."

"I'm not going to."

He filled her pussy, taking his time, making it last, going slowly, making love to her. When that wasn't enough, he moved her onto her side so that he could look into her eyes as he spread her thighs, sliding back in deep. The cock was still in her ass, not going anywhere. "You're all mine. This pussy is all mine." He began to increase his thrusts, going as deep as he could, and knowing in his heart, that he wanted to claim every single part of her, forever.

"Touch yourself, baby. Let me see you come. I want to feel it all over my cock."

He watched as she stroked over her clit. Her pussy tightened around him, making him groan, and he didn't stop with his thrusts. He kept up the pace loving the feel of her body opening up beneath him.

This was how it was always supposed to be. The two of them together.

"Come for me, Lola. Come all over my cock."

She fingered her pussy, and within seconds of his giving the command, she came over him, spearing him toward his own orgasm. He loved the squeeze of her pussy wrapped around him, and collapsed down beside her, panting for breath.

His cock still inside her, he held onto her.

Neither of them said a word as they caught their breath.

Sinner kissed her shoulder and stared around her bedroom. "This is totally you." It was light colors, feminine, and beautiful. "Why didn't you ever decorate our room like this?"

She chuckled. "You're a guy, and you're in an MC. I don't know. I just thought, you know, that you'd like dark colors. Blacks, browns, reds."

He laughed along with her. "Let me take this out." He eased the dildo out of her ass. "Come on. Let's go wash up." He pulled out of her pussy, taking hold of her hand, leading her toward the shower. While the water was heating up, he washed the dildo, and then followed her right into the shower. Taking the soap from her hands, he started to massage the lather against her pale skin. "You didn't catch enough sun."

"I was so busy. Computer work doesn't always allow me to go out in the sun."

"We'll have to rectify that, won't we?"

"Not right now. Fall is here, and winter is just around the corner. There is going to be no chance of us catching anything but death."

He wrapped his arms around her, settling his chin on her shoulder. "What about a sun bed?"

"They cause death," she said. "I'm fine. Honestly."

He handed her the soap, and she started to wash his body. He held his hands up, giving her unlimited access to him. When she slapped his ass, he playfully did the same to her, loving the little yelp of surprise.

"I love your juicy ass."

"I'd be careful if I was you. Your ass is getting just as juicy." She then further surprised him by giving his ass a little bite.

This is what she needs.

You both need this.

"Be careful with those teeth, baby. You bite, and I'm not afraid to bite back."

With her eyes glinting up at him, she bit his ass again. He caught her arms, hauling her up off the floor, and pressing her against the shower, and his body. "You're playing with fire, little miss."

"I may be playing, but I'm the one that has more bite than bark."

He stared into her eyes, and he couldn't read exactly what was going on in her head, but he knew she wanted to play, and seeing as they had been together for a couple of years, and she had never done this, he wanted to. He'd been wanting this for as long as they had been together.

Their lives were what brought them here, and he was going to see to it that their paths brought them back together again.

He caught her hands, locking them together with his. Leaning forward, he pressed a kiss to her neck, and then gave it a little nibble. "Is this what you're wanting?"

She shook her head.

"How about this?" He kissed down her body to her breast. The breaths she was taking suddenly got deeper. The points of her nipples hardened, and she pressed against his touch, clearly wanting him, needing him. Flicking the tip of her nipple, he watched as she closed her eyes. Her hands squeezed around his, and he knew he had her. "You like that?"

She nodded. "Yes."

"Good." He took her nipple into his mouth and

gave it a little bite. Moving across the valley of her tits, he went to her other one, and did the same. He loved when she cried out, and didn't fight to get away. If anything, she fought to get closer to him.

He teased her breasts, playfully nipping, biting, and licking. Sinking down to his knees, he nibbled on her rounded stomach, and then down, lifting one of her legs over his shoulder, opening up her sweet pussy. Pressing his lips against her clit, he sucked the hard nub into his mouth, loving the way she cried out his name, wanting him, begging for him.

"You want me, don't you, babe? You want my mouth on your clit."

"Yes. Please, Sinner."

Sliding his tongue across her clit, he gazed up, watching as she held onto the wall, trying to use it for support. He had released her hands a little while ago, so that he could hold her thighs and hips. Damn, he loved her body. It was so ripe, so ready to be fucked. He had spent many times, many hours, dreaming of having her swollen and pregnant with his kid. Even now, the thought of it had him hard as fucking rock. He was desperate to see her like that.

"Please, Sinner."

"Do you want to come, babe?"

"Yes, yes, please."

He smiled against the curve of her stomach. With a finger, he worked it inside her still tight pussy. Adding a second, and then a third, he sucked on her clit, giving it a little bite as he did. She loved a little bit of pain, and it was a revelation that was only now coming through. He fucked her pussy, licked her clit, and as he did, his cock got harder. Their time away had only made his feelings for her grow stronger.

"Sinner, please," she said.

Smiling against her slick pussy, he focused on her clit, and gave her the orgasm that she was craving. When it hit, he marveled at the power of her release as her cream flooded his fingers. He licked it up, savoring the taste of her.

When it was over, he stood up, licking his fingers. Her cheeks were flushed, and it had nothing to do with the warmth of the water.

"You taste so good."

She licked her lips and then sank to her knees on the floor.

"Lola, what are you doing?" he asked.

In all the time they had been together, Lola had tried to give him oral. It had always failed horribly. She hadn't been able to complete it and had often ended up in tears. It wasn't a good experience for either of them, and after it had happened twice, Sinner had stopped her from ever doing it again.

"Baby, you don't need to do this."

"I want to." She wrapped her fingers around his swollen cock. "I want to do this. I've been dreaming about it, Sinner. Being on my knees, holding your cock, tasting you. I want to try this."

"The other time—"

"Forget the other time. I don't care about that. I'm trying here. Please, Sinner, let me do this for you."

He saw in her eyes that she wanted to. Nodding his head, he watched as she looked at his cock. He was nervous. There was no denying it. Seeing Lola in tears, in any kind of pain was a turn-off to him. He didn't want to spoil their time together, but if this was what she wanted to try out, then he was more than willing to give it to her.

She ran her hands up and down his length, working from the base up to the root, then down again. Her touch set him on fire, in all the right ways. The feel of her hands drove him crazy. The arousal just built when he was with her. Everything else faded away, and could wait for another day.

Then she moved closer, and his heart seemed to stop as she flicked the tip with her tongue. She took a pearl of pre-cum. A second later, she covered the tip, and only took the tip of him, sinking a little more onto his cock. She pulled off and moaned. She fucking moaned, and not with disgust either. It was pleasure. She was enjoying it.

He wanted to fist pump the air, but instead, he held still as she continued to work his cock. Not only was he aroused because his woman was sucking his dick, but he was so proud of her. Each step they had taken this morning working its way into the evening had shown him that this time apart was essential. He hadn't wanted it to be true, but how could he not see the truth that was right in front of him?

She was growing stronger every single day, fighting her demons while he was finding himself again. After everything they had been through, this was what he needed to do, what he needed to search for, himself.

She took half of him into her mouth, stopping when she reached her hand. This time she didn't pull away from him. She began to bob her head, setting up a pace that was driving him closer to orgasm.

"I'm close, Lola."

He didn't want to ruin this moment by taking her by surprise. She didn't stop, and she kept on sucking his cock.

"Babe, if you don't stop, I'm going to come in your pretty mouth." She moaned in response, and it was just too much. The vibration from her mouth, and the pleasure of it on his cock, and he came, filling her mouth. She swallowed his cum, and kept on doing so until he was shaking from the pleasure. Finally, he pulled out of her mouth, sank to his knees, and stared into her eyes. Pressing a kiss to her lips, he wrapped his arms around her and held her close.

Once they had finished getting washed, he carried her back toward her bed, where they snuggled in.

"You've got to go soon, don't you?" she asked.

"Yes. I've got a friend who needs me."

She nodded.

He held her hand, bringing her fingers up to his lips.

"We've still got so much to do," she said.

"People to help, lives to change, and to grow." He agreed. He had to help Roxy, and he had to be there for Lucius. Sinner didn't know if the other man would care when Roxy passed, but something in his gut was telling him that Lucius would care, only he'd hide it. It was up to Sinner to make sure he found peace.

He pressed a kiss to her lips again, knowing that their time together was coming to a close.

"You know we could go back to Piston County. The two of us, and pick right back up where we left off," she said, sounding hopeful.

"We could do that without even a thought. We both know we could settle on that, babe. In a couple years, we'd be right back to the start, like we always are. We can't change who we are, or what we've become. Think about our future, Lola. I don't want a couple of years, or five or ten. I don't want to have to go through this again. I want forever with you. Don't you want that with me?" he asked.

"Of course, I do. I want it more than anything."

"Then know that I don't do this lightly. I'm not trying to be an asshole to you. I love you. That will never change. You were taken as a teenager, Lola, and you're a woman now. You need a chance to grow, and you can't do that with me breathing down your neck."

"This is not the happily ever after I envisioned."

"I know, babe, but this is how our happily ever after has to go for now." He pressed another kiss to her head.

When he made to pull away, she caught his hand, and tugged him close.

"Please, hold me. Don't go just yet."

He stared into her pleading eyes, and knew he couldn't deny her. Settling back down on the bed, he wrapped his arms around her as she moved, settling her back against his. Kissing her neck, he watched as the hours started to pass.

It took her a long time to fall asleep, and only when he was sure she wouldn't wake up, did he pull away. He took his clothes, changed in her sitting room, and then left.

Chapter Nine

One week later

Lola was finishing up the programing for a client who had found some problems in setting up his business. She spoke to him on the phone, at the same time she was connected to his computer, and was talking him through everything as well as fixing problems he'd created. It had been a week since she had last seen or even heard from Sinner. Her phone calls and text messages went unanswered, and she didn't want to worry.

So, she'd gotten in touch with Devil, and asked for him to get in touch with Sinner. It would seem that Devil also couldn't get in touch with him either.

Working was helping her try not to get distracted. At least, for the past week that was what she kept telling herself.

"Thank you so much, Miss Sparks. I appreciate all the help. Honestly, you're amazing."

"Just doing my job, sir. Do you need anything else for today?"

"No. I'm good."

"Have a nice day." She hung up the line, and immediately there was another call. She saw it was a little after two. Hunger, and the need for a break stopped her from answering another call. There were over thirty cubicles filled with experts like her.

How Whizz made her feel special was beyond her. She had to wonder if all of them were hackers, or just expert in reading computer code.

Her lunch was stored in her filing cabinet. She took it out, grabbed her jacket, and made her way down toward the cafeteria seating area. She took her lunch outside. The weather was cold but manageable. She stared up at the sky. There were blue skies, gray clouds, and just a feeling that it would be raining by the end of the day.

She chewed her sandwich watching the sky, all the time wondering about Sinner. He had sneaked out of her apartment.

The moment he moved away from her, she had woken up, and she had lain there, pretending not to hear him.

She closed her eyes, eating, not really tasting anything.

"You're deep in thought," Sarah said, disrupting her peace.

"I'm just thinking. It's nothing."

Sarah took a cigarette and lit it. "You don't mind, do you?"

Yeah, but what is the fucking point in telling you? You lit up anyway.

"It's fine." She finished her sandwich, and stared inside at the non-smoking zone. It was strange. Sinner was a smoker, not a heavy one, but she didn't find it offensive to be around him. Maybe it was just Sarah's complete lack of care. Why ask if someone minds *after* lighting up?

"I'm going to head in." She didn't wait to hear Sarah's response.

Entering the cafeteria, she went and bought herself a coffee, and took a seat in the corner.

Sipping at the hot liquid, she wondered about Sinner.

Putting her cell phone on top of the table, she texted Devil once again.

Lola: **Any news?**

Devil: **Stop worrying so much. I'm in contact with him. Sinner's battery died. He told me to tell you**

he'll be in touch.

Sinner's battery had died. Why not text from someone else's phone? She didn't say anything, and instead, went back to drinking her coffee.

"Hey, so I've got a question for you," Sarah said, taking a seat at the table opposite her.

"What kind of question?" Lola sipped at the hot liquid, really not caring about Sarah or her question.

There were loads of ways of getting in touch. Why didn't Sinner contact the club and then get them to tell her? She had been so worried about him, and he was fine.

He's part of a different club now. You can't keep expecting the same treatment. He's out there because you put him there.

"Well?" Sarah asked.

She shook her head, and frowned. "I'm sorry. What was the question?"

"I'm just curious about you. Your name came up in a search. You were taken from the streets, right? Kidnapped."

Lola stared at Sarah as she just spoke about a point in her life as if it was nothing.

"What do you want, Sarah?"

"It's true then? You're the Lola Sparks in those stories?"

She nibbled on her lip. Whizz had warned her that when she ventured out there was a chance that someone would find a story or remember it.

"I really don't want to talk about this, but yes, it's true. Don't tell anyone else, please?"

"Shit, yeah, I'm sorry." Sarah held her hands up. "I'm so sorry. I didn't … I thought it was you, but I didn't know it was. God, I'm such a bitch."

Lola stared across the table, and waited.

"How? Why are you here?" Sarah asked. "The story didn't say why that guy took you. Surely you could be doing anything."

"That guy took me because I had a knack for computers, Sarah. I used to be a hacker. This is all easy to me. I was a budding computer person, hacker, techno thingy, whatever. Don't believe everything that you read. Some of it is just made up bullshit."

"Is this why you don't date anyone?" Sarah asked.

"I don't date anyone because I'm still with someone. We're just having a break at the moment. Well, not a break. I saw him last week." She licked her suddenly dry lips. "I'm … doing what I need to do, okay? I would appreciate it if you didn't tell anyone."

"I've not told Belinda either. Look, I know I come across as some stupid bimbo, but I'm not. It's easier to have people believe that I'm useless, and that there's nothing inside, you know."

Lola stared at the woman that she had believed that very thing.

"You don't have to come out partying with us. I understand."

"I enjoyed going to clubs. It helped me."

"You can come anytime, and I'll stop Belinda from saying anything, and I will stop saying something as well. Wow, I was such a bitch."

She smiled. "Don't worry about it."

"I just want to be your friend," Sarah said. "Nothing else."

"How did you find out that information?" Lola asked. "It's not exactly easy to find."

"I want to write a story," Sarah said, smiling. "I know, weird, right? I love to read, and I've even started writing. I'm researching at the moment. I typed in some keywords, and your story popped up. I didn't dig or anything. It was just there, and then I had to ask." She pointed toward the window where they had been sitting outside. "I don't smoke often, only when I'm nervous. If you didn't like me smoking, just say so. Don't take anyone's crap, Lola. You don't have to."

Lola sat back in her chair, and looked at the woman opposite her, surprised by the kindness she was portraying.

"Thank you."

"Anytime. I better get back to work. I kind of sneaked out when I saw you leave. I wanted to talk to you in privacy." Sarah reached over and covered her hand.

Lola got the comfort that Sarah was trying to give her. It was sweet of her, and she appreciated it.

Thirty minutes of her lunch break had already passed. Her sandwiches were gone, and so was her drink. There was nothing left. She was about to leave when her cell phone rang.

It was Sinner's number.

She stared at it, wondering if she should even bother to answer. *Don't be a bitch.* This was what she had been wanting all week.

Taking his call, she sat back, waiting, then realized she needed to actually say something. "Hey."

"Babe, it's me."

She chuckled. "I know it's you. I've been freaking out about you to be honest. Wondering where you were."

"I'm fine. My battery died, and then we were on the road. I didn't see a problem. I know you were worried, but I don't want to check in with Devil every time I go somewhere else."

"I understand?"

"Do you? I'm part of the crew, but I'm not in Piston County anymore. If you don't hear from me, then you're going to have to be patient."

"What if something happens to you?"

"Devil will be alerted. It's not all bad, I promise. Nothing is going to happen."

"You charged your phone?"

"Yeah, and the moment I did, I had to go through all of the texts and missed calls."

"I'm sorry." She teased with a strand of her hair, which had come loose from the bun she had put it in. "I guess we're all learning these new barriers."

"I know. Being on the road is different. I caught up to Lucius and the others. We're heading down to the coast to do some partying."

She smiled thinking of Sinner dancing. He wasn't a very good dancer, but he had always tried for her. She wanted to be angry that he'd not been in touch, but why should she? They were in different worlds right now. Something *she* had started.

"What's going on with you?" he asked.

"Let's see, my friend, the one that I made, she knows about me, and about the kidnapping. She found it on some old news online," she said.

"How does that make you feel?"

"I don't know. At first I was stressed out, but now, I don't care. You know." She shrugged. "There's not a lot I can do. It's part of my life."

"If you worry, call Devil and Lash. They will help you out." Lash was the Prez of The Skulls.

"I will. I know the drill. I think I have their numbers on speed dial even before emergency numbers." She laughed.

She heard some commotion in the background, and she was a little jealous and envious. Glancing around the sterile and boring cafeteria, she wished she was with him, and not here alone.

Choices.

This had been *her* choice.

And look where it had gotten her. The day and night she spent with Sinner was one of the best experiences of her life so far. She would remember and cherish it always.

"I've got to go, babe. Take care."

She said her good-byes, and closed her phone.

He was fine, and she needed to realize that he would be. He didn't have to keep checking in every two seconds, just like she didn't need to. She was fine. She was happy, and she was safe.

****

"Your girl got you on a tight leash?" Lucius asked.

Sinner looked up to see Lucius with his arm wrapped around Roxy. The couple were standing on the beach, swaying to the music. It was warm where they were, which was a million miles away from where Lola was, experiencing the beginning change of fall. "Yeah." He pocketed his cell phone.

"Why haven't we seen your girl?" Rock asked. He was a long-term Nomad. Rock had tried to do the settling game with them in Piston County. It had lasted a day, and then he was gone. He never stayed in one place, and was always on the move. That was his thing, and that was how it was going to stay.

"You don't stick around, buddy. Maybe if you did, you'd know a thing or two."

"I know Devil's woman has the nicest tits I've ever seen," Rock said. "Of course, I wouldn't say that to Devil's face."

"Too late," Devil said, drawing all of their

attention toward the large man standing to the side of the group.

Sinner smiled as he caught sight of Pussy, Death, and Ripper. Each looked pissed off with him.

"Boys," he said.

"Wow, Devil, to what do we owe the honor of your visit?" Lucius asked. He pulled away from Roxy, and gave a bit of a bow.

"I decided I needed to do some hunting. You see, Sinner here made sure that his girl was to call me any time she needed some help. When her guy goes missing, guess who is the first person she calls?" Devil pointed at himself. "You didn't call."

"Devil, man, you're too late. He has already put a call in to his old lady. His balls have been snipped, and he can party right now as if he's a single guy," Rock said.

Devil shook Lucius's hand, and moved toward Rock. When Rock put his hand out, Devil slammed his fist against the guy's mouth.

Rock went down, and laughed. "Yep, yep, I deserved that. Shouldn't have said some bad shit about your girl, right, Devil?"

"If you need to ask that question, I didn't hit you hard enough."

Sinner got up off his ass, and held his hand out to Devil. His old Prez took him and pulled him in for a hug.

"Good to see you, Sinner. You're looking good."

"You're looking like shit."

"Lexie's preggers again," Pussy said. "I think we should have called Devil 'fuck-a-lot'."

"Or 'lots-of-cum'," Death said.

"'Baby machine', maybe?" Ripper asked. When the guys looked at him, he held his hands up. "Forgive me. I don't have all of your wisdom and words. I make this shit up as I go along."

"We all can tell that," Sinner said, laughing.

Ripper gave him the finger, and they all just laughed.

"Congratulations," Sinner said.

"Yeah, another kid to put through college," Devil said, but there was a smile on his face that told Sinner he was really happy with that.

"You're happy about it?"

"Yeah, of course I am. I just, Laurell was supposed to be the last. Lexie's exhausted, so I've decided that I'm going to take matters into my own hands. I'm going to get my balls chopped," Devil said. "Only way I can stop getting her knocked up. I can't keep my hands off her."

"Lexie's a good woman," Sinner said.

"You talked to yours?"

"I did. Just before you arrived. I let her know she shouldn't be calling you."

"Let's go for a walk. Give the other brats time to catch up."

Sinner followed Devil down toward the ocean. The tide was out at the moment.

"How have you been?" Devil asked.

"I've been doing good. Much better. I've got my shit together, you know."

"Have you seen Lola?"

"Yeah. I went to see her a week ago. I stayed the night."

"Do you think that is wise?" Devil asked.

"Yeah, it is. I still love her, and we'll be back in Piston County at some point."

"Relationships like these are hard, Sinner. Temptation is put in your way, will you even want to go back?" He nodded at the women around the club brothers. Roxy was by Lucius's side, and he saw the two were holding hands. Yep, that was going to be a problem.

"None of them are Lola, Devil. I know what I want, and what I don't want."

"I get that, son. Sometimes decisions are taken out of our hands, you know? What if she finds someone else?"

"Then I'd be the better man."

Devil laughed. "You're a better man than I am. I'd kill any bastard who tried to steal Lexie away."

Sinner laughed. "Of course, I'd make sure that Lola knew I wasn't going away without a fight. I love her, and that is never going to change. So, what are you doing here?"

"Making sure you're not dead."

"I'm part of the Nomad Chapter now. I can go days and weeks without a word."

"Yeah, but when I called Lucius and he hadn't heard from you, and you weren't in contact with Lola, I was concerned."

"Are you happy about Lexie?" Sinner asked.

"I'm … worried. Phoebe is around helping us out. Lexie is exhausted, and there's talk that she may need to rest during this pregnancy. It's not a problem. Simon can be a big help."

"And bribing him with Tabitha works just as well?"

"It gets the job done, and that's what I'm trying to do. Get the job done." He sighed. "Did you know I'm not the only one doing some bribery. Even Tiny's figured out the best way of getting our kids to do shit is to bribe her with time with Simon."

"That's what parents do, Devil. It's all about the bribery."

"I'm shitting myself to be honest. Lexie has told

me I've got to do the birds and the bees talk with him. I want him to know that most birds stay locked up in cages, and don't ever come out."

Sinner threw back his head and laughed. "For real?"

"I started fucking women at a young age. I do not want Simon to follow in my footsteps. Especially not with Tabitha."

"Maybe he'll get bored of waiting."

"I don't want to be a granddad."

"Then give him the protection talk." Sinner slapped him on the shoulder. "It can't be that hard, right?"

They headed back toward the rest of the group who were singing and dancing to a song playing out of someone's player on the cell phone.

Sinner didn't have any fancy shit on his phone other than a camera. He didn't do apps, or social media, or other crap. Roxy held her hand out to him, and together they swayed to the music.

"You're in a better mood," she said.

"You told him yet?"

The smile that was on her lips crashed down.

"I'll take that as a no."

"You can judge me all you want, Sinner. You don't know me, and you don't know Lucius."

"I know that he cares about you. He may not love you, but he does care, and that has feeling in as well."

"What are you two talking about?" Lucius asked, breaking in.

"I was just asking her about how her results are going."

Roxy shot him a glare. "I told him to mind his own damn business, and to stop spoiling the fun with crap that is not his concern."

He gave her the finger, and went to grab a bottle of beer from the stash that Rock had brought with him. Pussy and Ripper were dancing, pretending to be two girls, which was too funny. Sinner pulled his cell phone out and taped it. The moment they were done, he sent one to Sasha and the other to Judi.

The sun went down, and they kept on partying. Sinner and Rock went for food around seven, and even as the whole tide came in, they still didn't move from their spot.

He was having a buzz from the beer, and headed around one rock to take a piss when he paused.

"You okay, Roxy?" Lucius asked. "You'd tell me if something wasn't right?"

Sinner had thought Lucius and Roxy were both shit-faced from all the beer. Staring at them now from where he was standing, he saw they were very much fucking sober.

"I told you, I don't get my results for a little while. Everything is fine, Lucius. Don't worry."

Roxy made to move past Lucius. The brother caught her arms and pressed her against the wall. It wasn't hard, and there was no violence to it at all. Lucius cared about Roxy, and may have felt something more.

"You don't think I notice the change in you, Roxy? How weak you're getting? The way the cold is affecting you. Your loss of appetite. Don't try for a second to fool me, babe. It's not going to work."

Tears were in her eyes as she looked at him.

"It's back, right?"

She nodded, not saying anything.

"What do you have to do this time?" Lucius asked.

She shook her head.

"What?" There was real pain this time in Lucius's

voice.

Roxy started to speak, and then stopped, clearing her throat. "They can't do anything else, Lucius. That's it. I've done everything that I can do. I … I'm dying."

Sinner watched with tears in his own eyes as Lucius pulled her into a hug. They were best friends, he saw that now. Best friends, lovers, partners—they meant something to each other.

"How long?" Lucius asked.

"Lucius?"

"How long?" he asked with a bit more firmness to his voice.

"I'm on borrowed time now."

"No."

"I'm sorry. I … I wanted one more party with you. I won't see Christmas, and I won't see your next birthday. I won't see the New Year. At best, I'll make it to Halloween." The last one was said on a sob.

Sinner's heart broke for her, especially as he watched Lucius as well. The brother was just keeping it together. He held Roxy so damn tightly that it was just too painful to watch. Leaving them alone, Sinner headed out toward a private part of the beach. It was fucking cold, and he had his jacket on, wrapped around him.

"Life is fucking bullshit, right?" Lucius said, coming to sit down beside him. He had changed his beer for some whiskey. The scent was strong, overpowering. "You saw and heard that shit. Roxy told me that she told you. You're supposed to take care of me and help me through that kind of shit." Lucius laughed.

"You've known Roxy a long time?"

"Yeah. She's … like a best friend to me. Without fail she has always been there for me, and I've been there for her. The longest time I stayed in one place was to help her. I left home at sixteen, and I was on the road with my first bike by eighteen. Couldn't stand the same kind of people. They were all fucking rotten to the core. Knew Roxy as a kid. We stayed in touch. Memorized her fucking number." Lucius stopped, taking a long swig of his drink. "She has spent more of her life in a fucking hospital. I was her first fuck." Lucius stopped, and shook his head. "I knew life was unfair. I, this is cruel," he said. "She deserves better than this."

Sinner didn't say anything. There was nothing to say.

"She's going to die," Lucius said. "My little Roxy, she's going to die, and there's nothing I can do. She had plans. She wanted to be a wife, and a mother, and everything, and now she's going to have nothing."

Sinner took the bottle of whiskey from him and took a drink. He needed it.

"She's on borrowed time. There are rapists, murderers, child killers, and fucking molesters who will live long healthy fucking lives, and what does my girl get? Fuck all! Where is the fairness in that?"

Sinner shook his head.

"I'm a fucking monster. I've killed people without blinking an eye. Taken life without giving a fuck to what it means, and she has done nothing. She is an angel." Lucius, stopped, dropped his head between his knees.

The anger, the rage, it was coming off him in waves.

"I can't save her. For the first time in my life, I can't save her, and she's the only one in the world that deserves to be saved."

"I'm sorry."

Chapter Ten

Sinner: **Feeling really shitty right now.**

Lola: **Why?**

Sinner: **Miss you so much, and just, remembering stuff. You had every right to leave to do whatever it is you need to do.**

Lola: **What is going on?**

Sinner: **Just realized that life is way too fucking short right now.**

Lola nibbled her lip and wondered what else to say. The text had come through really late, which she didn't mind. She loved hearing from him. It was one of the highlights of her day.

Lola: **Do you need to talk about it?**

Her cell phone rang. "What's wrong, Sinner?"

"I just really needed to hear your voice."

"Are you crying?"

"No. I'm not crying. I've just spent most of the night out in the fucking cold, and I just got into my hotel room. I was spending time with Lucius, and we got talking, and drinking. Is it too late to talk?"

She glanced at her clock to see it was the early hours of the morning.

"It's fine. Talk away."

"Did you know Lexie was pregnant again?"

"No. I didn't."

"Devil's here. So are Pussy, Ripper, and Death. They came on a manhunt to make sure I hadn't died."

"Good. I'm glad. I don't want anything to happen to you."

"We were having a little party with the other Nomad club members. There's a few of them, and then there's Lucius and Roxy. Let's just say shit got real too fucking quickly."

She listened as he explained the relationship between Lucius and Roxy, and also Roxy's medical problem.

"That is awful."

"Yeah, Lucius isn't in the right fucking place right now. In fact, I'd say he's in a dangerous place. Kind of scary as well."

"Angel called me," she said when there was a lull in the conversation.

"She did?"

"Yeah, there's a erm, they're planning a get-together this Christmas. Some of the Chaos Bleeds and The Skulls. I was thinking of going. What about you?"

"You'd be there?"

"Yes, that's what I said. I would be there, and I'd love for you to be there as well. We could make a thing of it. You know, catch up? I'll get you a present as well."

"Call it a date, babe. I will be there."

"I'll let Angel know, or you can tell Devil. I really don't know how this all works. Will you even be allowed there as part of the Nomad Chapter?" she asked.

"I'm still me. Nothing has changed."

She smiled. "I'm glad to hear that."

"I'm sorry for calling you so late or so early."

"It's fine. I'll get up. Go for a walk or something."

They said their good-byes, and she lay back in her bed, thinking of Sinner, of his kindness, and his love.

It was strange. She had gone from being kidnapped by a monster, to finding solace with a bunch of men known for doing monstrous things. There was just something about The Skulls and Chaos Bleeds. They lived by their own code, and she had felt safe with them, safer than with anyone else.

****

The days passed without any event for Lola. Sarah was in fact a charming person when she wasn't being a bitch, but then any woman could be like that. Work continued to be exactly that, work. There was nothing inspiring about it. Clients phoned up, she handled their queries, sold them stuff they needed, and then helped them work through their mishaps.

The end of the day would roll around, and she would go and try something new. She had gone to different clubs with Belinda and Sarah. Had been the fifth wheel in a date. Had awkward moments when their dates brought dates.

She did her best to be upfront with the men. They were there because of their friends, and she was there because of her friends. Her heart, her body, and her mind were with Sinner. They talked often on the phone, and she knew he was going through a rough time right now. Being on the road and with Lucius wasn't being as much fun as she had hoped it would be for him. Roxy, the girl he had talked to her about, was not getting better, and was getting worse.

Even though she had yet to return to Piston County or even to Fort Wills, that didn't stop the regular visitors, including Whizz.

"You left that building looking really fucking bored," he said. They were sitting in café near where she worked. It was late, and she was tired, and hungry.

"It is a boring place. You'd look down your crooked nose at it. You wouldn't like it at all."

"Neither do you. You've got a shitload of potential. Why here?" he asked.

"You know why here, and you know that it's working, so stop trying to confuse me with your questions."

The waiter came to them, and they ordered their food.

"That is an improvement," Whizz said.

"What is?"

"For a long time, you allowed me to order for you. Now you ordered for yourself."

"A lot is changing. You probably don't really see it, but it's happening."

Whizz chuckled. "I see it."

"So, is Lacey alive or did you hide her body behind your tool shed or something?"

He sighed. "I got angry. She was still in the house. Sally and Daisy were out. I lost my temper, but I would never hurt her. We argued. That was all."

"Poor Whizz," she said.

"Yeah, poor me. She can't cook, and yet she keeps on trying."

"She just wants to look after you. One day Sally is going to fly the precious nest, and then who is going to cook your precious dinner?"

Whizz frowned. "Damn, I hadn't thought of that."

"Have you thought about *who* might take Sally away?" she asked, curious.

"First, no guy is going to be taking my girl away from the nest, not unless she wants to be taken," Whizz said. "Secondly, fuck, I've got to figure out how to find a decent cook."

She chuckled. "It's always fun being with you. Are you staying around for long?"

"Just long enough to try to convince you to get rid of this job. You don't need it. We both know you're better than this dull mundane crap," he said.

"You mean coding the website for Old Ladies MC clothing line?"

"That could be one thing, and another could be

hacking. That can still be a lot of fun. You could be in control of all of Chaos Bleeds security rather than leaving it to me."

She rolled her eyes. "You're exaggerating."

"I'm not. Why do you think I'm always visiting, huh? It's not that I don't like you, Lola, but I've got a life, too, and it's not at Piston County. I work hard for my club, and they're where my loyalties lie."

"What about when Simon and Tabitha grow up, get married, and have babies? Our clubs are coming together. You've got to see that."

"Two clubs, two different places, still need two of everything. Now, they already have two of everything."

"What about Butch?" she asked.

"What about him?"

"When are you going to stop punishing him, and you know, grow up?"

Whizz rolled his eyes. "None of your business. Butch has a life for himself in Vegas. That was long before you got involved with the clubs."

She blew a raspberry.

"You know that you've got shitloads of potential and you're wasting it on shitty businesses that will be closed down within the year. I could be training you. I could be helping you, and clean up those edges that make you sloppy."

"Hey!"

"I practiced."

"I know. Lacey's told me that she thinks you get turned on by computers rather than by her."

"She said that to you?"

Lola shrugged. "Does it?"

"No. Computers are life, okay? They're everything. Anyone who fights them is a loser."

"A loser?"

"Yeah. You can blow raspberries, I can call people and things losers."

It was always fun with Whizz. He never made her feel less of herself, or think about her own past.

"I want you to think about it."

"I will."

"I'm not asking you to try and lure you back to Piston County, or because anyone else has asked me to ask you. I'm asking because I know it's important. I know you can do it, and you love both clubs. We work together to protect each other."

"Sarah found out that information about me. Did you leave it for her to find?"

"There was media coverage over what happened, Lola. I can't control everything. There would be something somewhere. I didn't leave anything for anyone to find. This what you've got out here, this is all you. This is all that you've accomplished, no one else."

She smiled. "Well, I have to say, that does make me feel proud. I was wondering if you guys had been helping."

"Nope. I can guarantee that your sucky little life is all your own doing."

She rolled her eyes. "What exactly would you need me to do?"

Whizz leaned forward, and she followed him. "You'd be dealing with security. Checking Chaos Bleeds financials, dealing with companies, handling possible stock markets. The Skulls have taken several hits. Now that we don't deal with Ned Walker anymore, we have to bring in income. You could use your knowledge to help expand the website with the clothes thing."

"It's called fashion," she said.

"It's boring."

"Yeah, yeah, yeah, computers are the future."

"They're the present, you know that." Whizz chuckled. "You really do like to pretend you don't know what is going on, but you do."

"How is life at The Skulls?" she asked. Her entire world had been about computers. Her parents had gotten her a computer at the age of seven. That very first computer had been huge. There was no other word for it. She had gotten all As in her tests, and had even taken extracurricular classes to get it. One of her teachers had also told her parents that she excelled at computers and that it may even be worth the investment to get her a computer. Everything had been perfect. If only she had known that right at that moment, it would lead her to this moment.

It's not all bad.

You have The Skulls.

You have Chaos Bleeds.

You've got more friends and family than you've ever had in your entire life.

Without this path, you wouldn't have Sinner.

Just the thought of being without him in her life was enough to make her feel the pain. Every second of being in Andrew's torture was worth being with Sinner.

"It's fine. Lash is turning out to be a damn good Prez. He knew how to bring us out of all the illegal shit. We're legit, we've got income, the markets are doing fine. I keep an eye on them, and if there's anything that goes wrong, we can recover. It's only a small segment of our income, but it's enough to bring us in a nice little profit."

She nodded. "That's great."

"Have you gone and seen your parents yet?" he asked.

Her mind went completely blank.

"You haven't, have you?"

"It's not something I've been able to do yet."

Whizz stared at her for the longest time. "Do you even talk to them?"

"Yeah, I do. On the phone, you know. I don't want them to expect too much from me."

"You've got to forgive them."

"There's nothing to forgive." She forced a smile.

Whizz kept staring at her.

"What?" she asked.

"They're your family, Lola. They were out searching for you just like us. It's not like you didn't have anyone."

"The whole time I was with them, they were staring at me like was some bug under a microscope. I wouldn't have gotten such detailed looks if I was a monster in a fucking zoo," she said. It had hurt her more than she had let anyone know. Tears sprang to her eyes, and she was angry with crying. She didn't want to cry.

Crying was a weakness, and she was sick of it.

Wiping away her tears, she looked anywhere and everywhere but at him.

"It hurt?"

"Of course, it did." She laughed. "My own parents looked at me like I was a freak."

"You ever thought that they may have been looking at you out of fear."

She frowned. "What? I wasn't going to do anything to them. They had nothing to fear from me."

"Or maybe they were scared that if for a second they turned their backs on you, you'd take matters into your own hands." He gave her a pointed look, and she frowned. "Lacey had a lot of bad shit happen to her."

She knew what had happened to Lacey. They had spoken openly to each other late one night not long after Lola had recovered and left her parents. Lacey had been ganged raped, beaten, and nearly killed. She had been a young child, not even a teenager yet.

"I know about Lacey," Lola said.

"Lacey tried to end her life multiple times," Whizz said. "For a long time, she couldn't handle the memories. I'm not saying she was weak. We all deal with this stuff in our own way. Me, I pressed weights. I threw myself into my work. You, you hid from it. It was like you pushed it to the back of your mind, and slowly, you're processing it. Like a computer."

She smiled. "I'm mechanical?"

"No. If you were mechanical, you would have shut down already from being overloaded."

"What do you think I should do?"

"I think you should give your parents a chance. They still love you, and you love them."

"I'm not ready," she said.

"Then you've got to give yourself more time. You're stronger than you realize. I only hope that you can see that."

****

"There is way too much pussy here, and none of them are Sasha," Pussy said, taking a large gulp of his beer.

"You're not even interested?" Sinner asked.

In the past, Pussy had been all about fucking, sex, and licking pussy. If there was a woman willing, Pussy would be there. Now though, he was epitome of monogamy.

"Not at all. I tell you, Sasha is all mine. No other man has been with her, and I fucking love her. Besides, she'd probably beat me with a cast iron skillet if I stepped out on her, not that there is any chance of that," Pussy said, laughing. "My dick has one name, and one name only, Sasha."

Sinner laughed along with him, and took a drink of his beer. Ripper was in fact on the dancefloor with Roxy. The two had hit it off, and were getting along really well.

What Sinner had come to see was that Roxy was one of those women that drew people to her. It wasn't sexual. She was simply a nice woman, a kind woman. He liked her, and after witnessing Lucius's breakdown, he knew that it would affect his friend greatly. Glancing down the bar, he saw the man in question drinking straight from the scotch bottle. They had been riding up and down the coast for the past couple of weeks, and he still hadn't changed. Every time they settled down, he drank his way into oblivion.

No one could reach him, and after the first night, no one even tried.

"You have some serious moves," Ripper said, collapsing against the edge of the bar. "My wife would adore you. Maybe one day you could stop by Piston County and meet her."

The smile on Roxy's face slipped a bit. "Yeah, maybe one day that would be fun."

"Excellent. I'm just going to go and check in on her and our kids." Ripper pulled out his cell phone, and made his way out of the club.

"Can you believe how different we all are?" Pussy asked.

"How do you mean?"

"Years ago, we would have had several of these bitches eating out of the palm of our hand. Now, it's all different. The only woman I want is Sasha. You're taken. We're all taken in our own little way." Pussy took a long drink of his beer.

"Do you ever miss it?" Sinner asked. "Do you ever long to take one of those women around the back of the bar, and fuck her until she can't remember her own name?"

Pussy shook his head without even looking at the dancefloor. "None of them are like my Sasha. She trusted me when no one else would, and to me, that's better than anything in the world. I love her more than anything. Just thinking about her, I can't stop smiling." And there was indeed a smile on his face. It was a large one as well, kind of scary. "Think about it. Sasha couldn't see a fucking thing. She was blind. There was no way of her knowing who she was marrying. I could have been fucking ugly, evil to the core, and yet she would touch my face, and I would feel utterly different. She trusted me out of everyone in her life, and that, I will never forget."

"Hey, what's her mother doing lately?" Sasha's mother had been addicted to drugs, booze, and prescription meds while her then-husband, Sasha's stepfather had been hurting her. When Chaos Bleeds learned the truth, they'd helped her, got her into rehab.

"She's seeing some rich millionaire out in England, last I heard. Sasha writes to her, and I listen to the letters. I don't think there is much love lost between mother and daughter." Pussy's phone blinked, and Sinner watched as he pulled it out, and the smile on his face was so endearing. "They can't wait for me to come home." He tilted his phone for him to see the picture of a cake, Sasha, and Shay getting bigger by the day. The smiles on their selfies was so endearing that it made Sinner pause, and wish that was what he was getting.

"I've got to go and take a leak," he said.

Finishing his drink, he made his way out of the bar, around the back toward the darkened alley. Grabbing his cell phone, he dialed Lola's number. They were both on this journey together, but it didn't stop him from loving her, not one bit. Their time apart was essential, but he missed her so much.

Moments like these when he had his club brothers with him who were sharing pictures that he wished he had, he missed her. The house, the kids, the life, he wanted it all.

She picked up on the third ring. "Hello."

In the background, he heard a lot of noise. "Where are you?" he asked.

"Oh, sorry, it's a party. Only it's a house party. I thought it was going to be a small event, but it's feeling more and more high school. Hold on a sec, I'm just grabbing my jacket and heading out."

Even though she was at a party and not at home, he couldn't help but smile. She hadn't been able to handle the Chaos Bleeds parties without freaking out.

"It's so cold," she said. He heard more noises that sounded like her putting on a jacket, and then she was walking. The noise soon went quiet. "There, all better. Hi, Sinner." She giggled. "How have you been?"

"I'm doing great. Believe it or not, I've just come out of my own party. Well, it's a nightclub, but several of the guys are here. You started a Sinner hunt."

"Really? Who's there?"

"Devil, Ripper, Pussy, and Death. They must have already been on the road by the time that I called you."

"I cannot believe him. He told me that you had your own life to lead, and that he couldn't keep track of you."

"Ah, the thing about Devil is, he pretends not to care, but deep down, he's a big softie. Of course, you betray him, and he will shoot you in the head, merely for the fun of it."

"Right, I must remember that."

"Yes, you must."

Again, she laughed. "It's so good to hear from you. I know it has only been a couple of days, but I really like hearing your voice."

"I miss you, too, baby. It was really weird to be honest. I was sitting at the bar chatting with Pussy. Asking if he missed chasing around women—"

"Do you miss it?"

"No. Not at all. I'm more than happy with what we've got, babe. What about you?"

"I never chased boys. I've got one man I'm interested in, and I'm speaking to him right now."

The smile was not coming off his face anytime soon. "So anyway, I was asking him if he missed it, and being Pussy, of course not. Let's face it, he's completely devoted to Sasha. If he was ever going to step out on her, it would have been years ago, when they first got together, and he realized how hard it was for her. Then a picture came on his phone. Sasha and Shay. They had made him a cake, telling him they were excited for him to come home, and it got me thinking, do you want kids?"

"Do I want kids?"

"Yeah, little Lolas and Sinners running around."

"I hadn't thought about it. I didn't know you wanted kids?"

Just the thought of Lola swollen with his kid had him hard as fucking rock. He couldn't help it. The two of them, together. "We'd have to move out of our apartment, you know. Get a nice big place. Maybe something near to Devil and Lexie. Our kids could play."

"They wouldn't be short of partners and playing."

"No, they wouldn't." He chuckled, thinking about the next generation of Chaos Bleeds. Everything was changing, and he never thought he'd enjoy how fast it was moving, but he did. He didn't want to get off that train of movement and change. He wanted to jump right back on, and be there with Lola and with his club.

"Boys or girls?" she asked.

"Either. I wouldn't care. Do you think I'd be a good dad?"

"You'd be the best, Sinner. Everything you do, you do in the best possible way. You shouldn't doubt yourself one bit."

He heard her sigh, not a heavy one either. She sounded happy. "Are you okay, babe?"

"I had a talk with Whizz. It was … hard."

"You and Whizz conversed and you found it hard? How is that even possible?" He wasn't jealous of Whizz and Lola's relationship. When they had first rescued her, she had needed someone to talk to. Someone who knew exactly what she was going through, and that hadn't been him, or anyone else. Whizz understood her, and he had been able to reach Lola, and bring her back into herself, in a way that Sinner hadn't been able to.

"He thinks I need to go and see my family."

"What do you think?"

"I think there's a reason I didn't go and see them, and I don't want to go and see them."

He knew all about the reasons why she didn't want to see them, and it broke his heart. She avoided them as much as possible.

"This is about you growing, and about you finding yourself once again, babe. You and I both know what you need to do."

"I know what I *need* to do. It doesn't mean that I like it."

He laughed. "So, you're going to go and see your parents?"

"One day. Not yet. I'm not ready. I'm not sure at

all. Ugh, why do I have to do this? I don't want to do this, not at all."

Sinner knew she was going to do it. Every time she hated something, she would list a million and one reasons as to why she hated it, and yet she would go and do it anyway.

"You're laughing at me, aren't you?"

"Just a little, but that is only because I think you're cute."

She blew a raspberry. "I wish you were here."

"Funny you should mention that, because I was wishing that you were here."

"I love you, Sinner."

"I love you, too, babe. I'll let you go take care of stuff."

She sighed. "Okay, fine."

He disconnected the call. Just hearing her voice made him feel better.

Chapter Eleven

A couple of days later
Piston County

Devil stood in the main building of his wife's fashion shop. She was serving a customer, and looked so damn cute. She was wearing one of the dresses, something that nipped in the waist and flared out over her hips. What he loved was how it showed off her amazing tits and cleavage. He loved her tits, and even though they had nursed their kids, they belonged to him, just like every single part of her did.

The moment she saw him, she smiled, and left the serving counter. "It is good to see you. I didn't know you'd be here."

"I just got back in. The guys have gone to their homes looking for their women, and I knew you'd be here."

"Are you good to keep an eye on things?" Lexie asked, looking toward Natalie.

"Yep, I've got this." Natalie was sitting on a chair, a sketchbook in hand, and she was going at the sheets like crazy.

"Every woman who walks in here is inspiring Natalie. She's creating our next line just by imagining what the women would like. She's a machine."

"Sounds very busy."

"It is. It always is." They entered the back-room office where little Laurell was sound asleep. Jessica had David on her knee as she was reading to him.

"Slow day at the nurses' office?" Devil asked.

Jessica was a nurse who had helped to save Judi's life. She was also Snake's old lady, but it wouldn't have mattered. Devil would have made sure Chaos Bleeds was respectful to Jessica.

"You know it. Since this mysterious MC club has decided to go legit, we don't have to worry about any kind of serious injury," Jessica said, teasing. "Nah, I'm on a break, and seeing as Snake had to work at that sex club you've got going…"

"It's Naked Fantasies! Not a sex club."

"Women have their tits out, and earn money shaking their ass."

"Still not a sex club," Devil said. "I tell you, I've been to a sex club, and I know—" Lexie covered his mouth.

"He knows that if he wants to keep his man parts, he will keep talk of all other women out of it. I don't want to hear who came before me, babe," she said.

Devil stayed silent.

"I'm guessing you two want privacy." Jessica lifted David up, and when she made for Laurell, Devil shook his head.

"I've got her."

"Okay. I'll leave you two."

The door closed seconds later, and Lexie suddenly sat down in a chair.

"Babe, you need to go home, and we need to employ a nanny."

"A nanny, no thanks," she said. "I can look after my kids, thank you very much."

He saw the perspiration on her brow. She looked exhausted and close to collapsing.

"This is not me being nice about this, babe. This is me telling you that we're going to get a nanny, and you're going to fucking rest. We've done this before."

"And I'm fine. I can do this, Devil."

"Babe, nothing has changed for me. I'd rather have you than any of the kids we've had, okay? I love you. You're my entire world. Don't argue with me."

"I don't want to argue, but this is our family."

He leaned in close and kissed her head. "This is going to be our last one."

"Devil?"

"No arguments. I've already gotten it arranged. Jessica is helping as well. This is going to be our last kid, Lexie. No more playing around."

Laurell began to whimper, and Devil walked over to the small crib and smiled down at his little girl.

"How is Sinner?" Lexie asked.

He picked Laurell up, cradling her close. She was getting to be such a big girl now. So cute. He didn't like having so many daughters. The thought of the men in years to come was enough to make him nervous. He had a lot of experience with killing people, and using all kinds of weapons. He even knew how to dispose of the body as well.

"Sinner's doing well. His usual self to be honest."

"Do you think he'll be coming home anytime soon?"

"I don't know. He's … different."

"In what way?" she asked.

"It's hard to say exactly. I think the past few years it has put a strain on all of the guys, you know. With Lola it has made him face the fact that he has changed. Being out on the open road, it is helping him to deal with shit that he's been putting aside."

"I missed you."

He smiled over at his wife. "I do believe he'll be coming to Fort Wills with us for Christmas."

"Yeah, why are we going to The Skulls clubhouse for Christmas?" Lexie asked, with a smile on her lips.

"Don't give me that look."

"You see, I think a certain son of yours struck a

deal."

Devil rolled his eyes. "I told Simon that if he got the highest marks in his class in everything, then I would allow him to spend some time with Tabitha over the festive season."

"And?"

"His teacher told me that she is utterly surprised by the transformation in Simon. He is a model student. I arranged it with Tiny."

"How is Tabitha doing in school?"

"Great, I think. She's not as big a concern as Simon."

"Thank you," she said.

He smiled. "You told me you wanted Simon to have more options than you were given. He's going to do well in school, probably end up in college, in the city as some loser billionaire, and you know what? I'll handle it, because I'm the best dad in the world."

Laurell gurgled.

"See. Tell Mommy that I'm the best dad in the world."

"She doesn't need to tell me. I know it."

****

I want to go home.

This is so boring.

Yeah, I told you that you deleted like half of your stock footage.

Wow, could this day get any worse?

"Did you have a backup?" Lola asked. She listened to the man on the line, and she was so bored. It may be time to do something different with her life. She could have easily hacked into the guy's server, and found exactly where he kept his damn stock photos, but he was too busy moaning on the line.

She couldn't help but think of her phone call the

other night with Sinner. Not the one where they were both at parties, but the one where they got to talk, and play. She missed his hands, and it wasn't the same stroking her own clit, while hoping that Sinner would magically appear.

Lola wished that she could magically appear in front of Sinner. The problem was, he really did move around. Rarely was he in the same place at all. Devil was sending him money, and she knew that he was traveling with a group of men.

Sinner told her everything.

"Hey, girlfriend," Belinda said, pulling a seat along with her as she moved into her space.

"Hey to you, too."

"So, I was wondering if you'd be up for another party later."

"Nope. I just want to go home. Have a bit of quiet time I think." *Try not to think about my parents.*

They had left her a message as well. She always made sure to call when they were out of the house. Even this far away from them, she knew their schedule. Talking to them directly on the phone was awkward, even more so when she was in front of them, and having to make eye contact.

Deep down, she knew Whizz and Sinner were right. There was no denying it. They were both right, and she needed to do it, but right now, she just couldn't handle seeing them.

"Yes, sir. I'm sorry, sir. That's the file, correct. Okay then, have a great day."

She hung up the phone, and rested her head on the desk.

"Wow, that is the first time I've ever heard you lose your temper with a customer," Belinda said. "I hope you're not losing your touch."

"I'm not. Believe me, I'm not. I'm just over people and their problems already. I want to go home, and sit down, and relax, and pretend everything is fine with the world." She stared at the clock, and willed it to be five o'clock. Sometimes she stayed over, and got some overtime in. That was so not going to happen tonight.

"Are you looking for a new job?" Belinda asked.

"I don't know. I once had a job. A great one that I gave up to come here on my little problem solving mission." She air quoted the end part of her statement. Lola was so pissed off, and angry, and fed up.

"I need a coffee." She got up from her chair, and made her way over to the coffee machine. Her eyes hurt, and her temper wasn't getting any better.

The coffee didn't help, so she worked through the rest of the day, really pissed off, and angry. She turned down offers of a drink from Sarah and Belinda. There was only one thing she wanted to do, and that was go home, eat, shower, jump into bed, and read a good book, or maybe watch a sappy love story.

She was leaving her building when she paused to see Sinner standing there waiting for her. There was no sign of his bike, and for a second, she wondered if she was seeing things. This had to be the best way to end her shitty day.

"You're not going to come and give me a hug?" he asked.

Lola didn't care if they were being watched. She rushed toward him, and threw her arms around his neck, hugging him tightly to her. "How did you know?" she asked.

"How did I know what?" He held her so close, and she basked in his scent, in his touch, in everything.

"That I needed to see you?"

"I needed to see you, and I knew you wouldn't have a clue where to find me."

She pulled back just enough to stare into his eyes. "That's because you're always moving. You see, when you're in the same place, there is no fear of that, because you're in the same place."

"But I like surprising you, and I can keep on doing that because I move around, and I know where to find you." He pressed a kiss to her lips, and everything faded away. "You had a bad day?"

"The worst, and I was thinking of you, and this is perfect. Can you come home with me?" she asked.

"Yeah, I can come home with you." He took her hand, and together they made their way over to her car.

Climbing behind the wheel, she watched as he pushed the passenger seat back.

"I've only had Sarah and Belinda in the car. I don't like driving all that many people," she said.

"These people small?"

"A little bit, yeah." She chuckled. Starting up the car, she pulled out of the parking lot, and started the short drive home. "Usually I walk. I actually walk more here than I do everywhere else. However, with it being so cold and miserable, I sometimes take my car."

"I hate to say this to you, babe, but this car is a pile of shit."

"You would know. I bought it at a bargain price. I figured I'd only be driving short distances, and I could handle that." She shrugged. "I could have gotten a bike."

"Not a chance. You wouldn't have been able to handle it."

She gasped. "I'm offended."

"It took you a long time to let me drive you, remember?"

Lola nodded. She had rarely ridden with Sinner,

preferring either a car, or to walk. The back of his bike always looked so dangerous. "Maybe one day you'd take me out for a ride?"

"Maybe." He gave her a wink, and it warmed her from the inside out. "Are you going to quit?"

"I'm thinking about it. I really am. It's tiring work. I don't know. The customers today were just really pissing me off. They were not listening, and I found that so annoying, so irritating." She pulled into the parking lot for the apartment building. "We are here."

It didn't seem right to call this place home. They both knew it wasn't.

Within minutes they were in her apartment, and Sinner had her pressed against the door the moment it closed. He captured her hands, lifting them beside her head. His lips were on hers, ravishing her mouth.

She moaned, arching up, kissing him with the same passion that he had given her. Her body heated, wanting him more than anything.

"I couldn't go another second without kissing you," he said. He released her hands, and she still held them beside her head. His fingers stroked the collar of her shirt, and trailed down the center over her buttons.

Her nipples hardened, and she licked her suddenly dry lips. When he made no move to do anything, she reached for his belt. Tugging it open, she stared into his eyes the whole time.

"What are you doing?" he asked.

"Exactly as I want to. Don't hold back, Sinner. Do to me what you want to do. I'm not going to break. I'm a strong girl. I can take it."

He grabbed her shirt and tore it open. Another tug had buttons flying all around the room.

She pulled his shirt over his head, and marveled at all of the ink on his body. She saw her name near his heart, and once again, she was struck by how much she loved him. Sinner had marked his body with her name. She traced her finger over the ink. Unable to hold back, she smiled. "You still have it."

"You're still mine, Lola. That hasn't changed."

She went to her knees before him, pulling down his jeans until they were pooled at his feet. He stepped out of them, kicking them across the room and out of the way. He ran his fingers through her hair, dislodging the pins that were keeping it secure on top of her head.

Once she had his cock in her hand, she flicked the tip of his cock, and then covered it with her mouth.

He hissed, the sound echoing around her apartment.

"Fuck, baby. Give a guy a warning."

She pulled off his length, and smirked up at him. "I held your dick. What more warning did you need?"

He grabbed her hands and pulled her over his knee. He was on his knees, and had one foot on the ground, which he bent her over. Suddenly, he gave her ass a slap.

The burn warmed her ass, and went straight to her clit. She cried out his name, and wriggled against his knee. He slapped her ass again, and she loved it. Her pussy went slick, and she reached for his cock again.

"You like that, baby? You like being told off for being naughty."

She glanced up at him, seeing the concern in his eyes. "Feel me, Sinner." She opened her thighs for him, and he slid a finger between her swollen folds.

He pushed a finger inside her, and she groaned, wanting more. It wasn't enough, never enough.

"What is it you do to me?" he asked.

Sinner pulled his fingers from her pussy, and she eased off his leg. "It's exactly what you do to me." She wrapped her arms around his neck, and held him close. They were both naked, his hard, muscular chest completely different from her soft one.

He ran his hands up and down her back, gripping her ass.

Pulling away from him, she took his hand and moved him toward the sofa.

"I don't even get the chance to go into the bedroom." He took a seat, and she smiled at him.

"I've spent many nights sitting in that very place, thinking about you. Every time I do, I think about everything I want to do to you, and I'm going to show you now." She went to his jeans, and pulled out a condom. "You're always prepared."

****

Lola was the same person, but she was so different. Not in a bad way either. The woman before him was filled with so much confidence that it was turning him the fuck on just watching her.

Wrapping his fingers around the length, he watched her, amazed at what a beautiful woman she had become. She was no longer that scared little mouse.

She dazzled him with her smile and made him ache in ways that the old Lola never had.

"I'm always prepared."

He couldn't look away as she tore into the condom and removed the latex. She went to her knees before him and slowly began to slide the condom over his length. "You know, we don't have to do this," he said.

"I've not been to see the doctor for my shot."

"I was bare the last time I was inside you."

She smiled. "I think we're safe. I've had a period since then."

"What about those kids?" he asked.

"I thought we would start them when we were both back in Piston County."

"You do want kids?"

"With you, yes. I want kids. I want to have that life with you that we've talked about all the time."

"Have you gone to see your parents yet?" he asked as she straddled his lap. He held onto her plump ass. He was in no rush to get her pregnant, but he loved how open she had become with him.

"Nope, and I don't want to talk about my parents." She reached down, holding his cock, and then lowered herself over his length.

She sank down, and they both released a little gasp as she took him to the hilt. She sat on him, wrapping her arms around his neck.

He stared up into her eyes, knowing with all of his heart, that what they were doing was the right thing. They were going to make a better future for each other.

"Is this what you wanted?" he asked, squeezing her ass, lifting her up on his cock, and then pulling her down so that their bodies slapped together.

"Yes."

"You want this? You want to fuck me, baby?"

"Yes."

"Then ride me. Ride my cock because it belongs to you. It always has."

She held onto his shoulders, and she started to rock on his dick, taking him in deep. Her pussy squeezed him as she slid up and down his length. He watched her tits bounce, and then his cock as it disappeared inside her body.

Releasing one cheek of her ass, he teased a finger between her folds, touching her clit. The moment he stroked that swollen nub, she screamed his name, and her cunt tightened around him like a fucking fist.

She lifted herself up so that only the tip of his cock was inside, and slammed back down. She did this over and over again. All the time, he stroked her clit, bringing her closer to orgasm with each flick of his finger.

"Please, Sinner."

"You want to come?" he asked.

"Yes, yes, I want to come."

He pulled her off his cock and moved so that she was over his face.

"Sinner?"

"I want to eat your pussy while you suck my cock. I bet this was part of your fantasy." He moved her in such a way so that when she leaned over, she could reach his cock. Her pussy was soaking wet. He plunged his tongue inside her cunt, tasting her.

She removed the condom from his cock. He felt her lips on his cock, licking the entire length. He growled against her pussy, using his teeth on her clit, stroking from her pussy up to her clit, then down again, sliding inside her.

Sinner had been wanting the taste of her pussy for so long, it was like an ache, a yearning.

"You taste so fucking good," he said, then sucked her clit into his mouth.

She bobbed on his cock, taking him to the back of her throat, where she sucked his cock in deep, before releasing him. She used her hands and mouth on his dick.

With two fingers inside her pussy, he flicked her clit, feeling her orgasm start to build just as his own was.

They came together, the scent of sex heady in the air. He licked the cream from her cunt as she milked him dry, taking everything he had to offer and then some.

She swallowed every drop of him.

When it was over, he moved her so that she was

at the side of him, and he had his back that would hit the floor first if he fell off.

"Do you like my feet?" she asked, seconds later.

He laughed, and finally sat up, and she snuggled in close.

"I didn't expect it to end like that," she said.

"You didn't like my mouth on your pussy?"

"I loved it." She turned to look up at him. "I just love being with you."

He was struck once again by her natural beauty. Lola was always one hundred percent natural with him.

"I'm not going to be able to make another visit before Christmas," he said.

The smile that had been in her eyes seemed to fade. "Oh, of course, these are just a bonus."

"I want to help a friend out. I'll be at Fort Wills for Christmas, and I will even have a Christmas present for you," he said.

"I've already got one for you. I picked it out a few weeks ago. I'm hoping you'll love it."

"I love anything by you, you know that." He kissed her head. She stroked a finger over her name. He took her hand, locking their fingers together.

"Do you think you'll be able to settle down after being on the road again? I remember Lexie once told me that Chaos Bleeds were always on the road. You never settled down."

"We didn't. We'd ride from place to place, causing trouble where we could. None of us had dreams of settling down."

"What changed?"

"We got to see The Skulls, and how they had found a life together in one town. Not only that, Devil was trying to find his son, and then of course, he met Lexie, couldn't be without her, and some of us guys decided to take this kind of road as well."

"But there are still some that decided to stay as nomads?" she asked.

"You got it. I'm with a bunch of men right now. They're good men, but they would ruin everything the club has built up at Piston County." They really would. Just thinking about Rock and Lucius was enough to make his head spin.

They didn't believe in conforming, and Devil wasn't interested in keeping men down when they wanted to fly.

"I guess I just find it hard to believe that you'll be able to settle down so long after you've been away."

"What about you? Do you see yourself back in Piston County? This can go both ways, you know that? You've had your life away from the clubs, and from one town. Does the city life agree with? Does being without me agree with you?" he asked. He had to know these things, and he wanted her to know that she could talk to him, openly and honestly.

"I see us back in Piston County together, growing old together." She squeezed his hands. "Do you hate me?"

"I thought we had talked about this, babe?" he asked. "I don't hate you at all. In the beginning I was hurt, but now, with what we're experiencing together, there is no way I could hate what you're doing. You're a strong woman, and I love you. We've both got places to be, and one day soon, we'll join up with each other."

When he had left, Roxy had started to get worse. The reason he didn't think he was going to get the chance to be with Lola again was he didn't know how long he was going to be with Lucius.

The brother really wasn't taking her illness all that well. Roxy had warned him, and now that they were seeing the effects, Sinner knew something bad was going to happen.

"How about we not fight about the future, and we just bask in the now." He held her close, knowing that he would go fucking crazy if he ever lost Lola. They were apart right now because of *her* choice.

If he ever had her taken away from him, he would lose his shit, and it would fucking kill him.

"I want lots of kids," she said, suddenly.

"What?"

"When we have kids. I want lots of them. A whole houseful like Lexie. I want to be a good mother."

"You'd be an amazing mother."

****

Natalie tilted her head to the side, and admired the dress in the mirror. Old Ladies MC clothing was shut, but there was one dress that she had made with herself in mind, and she had never tried it on. Always been nervous about doing so. Being alone, with no fears of anyone coming in the shop, she gave a little twirl.

Her hair was piled high on her head. The chest area was designed to push breasts together, creating a nice cleavage. She had always been a bit of a boy, preferring jeans and long shirts. Working on a ranch never gave her much time or excuse for dressing up like a lady or a woman.

"You look beautiful," Slash said, making her gasp and turn toward him.

"Hey, I didn't hear anyone come in."

"I came around the back. I have a key." He held up his key, and gave her a smile. "You're trying on the merchandise."

"I'm going to pay for it. I'm just, I don't know. I feel silly." She gripped her hands, and smiled at him. "I made this for me."

"I know. I saw the drawing. I was surprised you never modeled for it. It's perfect for you."

"It makes me feel like a woman."

His gaze ran down her whole body. "Hate to say this to you, but you really are a woman."

"Why are you so nice to me?" she asked.

"What?"

"You don't know me, and I know you've got a club full of women, not to mention everyone in town that wants you. Why are you being nice to me?"

"I like you. Does there have to be a reason?" he asked.

"I'm not used to people sticking around because they like me, Slash. They come and go as they please. I'm no one important, and I'm selling the ranch to the club."

"This is not about the ranch, or wanting you for a reason, or any shit like that. I'm not the kind of guy who does shit like that."

She tilted her head to the side, and looked at him. "Then why? I know that Butler likes spending time with me, and watching me draw. Lexie thinks I'm funny. Paris has her reason, but I don't know why you do."

Natalie liked Slash a lot, and he was there. Butler had warned her that Slash had feelings for her, and like all guys, it had made her nervous. Was he expecting something from her?

He spent so much time with her, and she had truly believed he was her friend.

Slash stepped close to her, and she couldn't help the gasp that left her. He cupped her cheek, and tilted her head up so that she was staring into her eyes.

"I think you're the most beautiful woman I have ever seen. Yes, I want you, and no, I'm not going to rush you, or tell you that you need to make a choice." He kissed her lips with such tenderness that it surprised her. "I want to warn you though. Butler's lying. He wants you just as much as I do."

She was nervous.

No man had ever wanted her before, and now there were two.

She licked her dry lips, nervous, kind of scared.

"This changes nothing," he said.

It did though.

It changed everything.

Chapter Twelve

October

Most of the group that Sinner had started with had long since dispersed and gone their separate ways, and he had stayed with one man, one person. Rock was still around, and so was Roxy—only there was a problem. She was getting sicker by the day, weaker.

Lucius had wanted to take her home, only to find out that Roxy had sold her home, and had cut off all ties to the world she once knew. She was alone, and no one was there to help her.

"I don't want to keep taking her to hotels," Lucius said late one night. "She deserves to have some place to rest, and I can't give her that here."

"Where do you want to go?" Rock asked.

"Anywhere that is not here, okay?"

"You can have my old apartment," Sinner said. "In Piston County. You'll be near the club, and she'll be safe."

"What about your girl?"

"Don't worry about it. I want Roxy to have everything she needs."

"To die," Lucius said, forcing out a laugh. Silence fell after the sound disappeared.

"We know you care for her," Rock said.

"Yeah, well, caring for her didn't get me nowhere fucking fast, did it!" Lucius shook his head.

"I know you don't want to lose her."

"It doesn't matter what I want. The apartment is good. I'll talk to her about it, and then let you know."

Lucius got to his feet and left.

Sinner took another long swig of his beer, and stared out over the night sky. It was fucking freezing, but he didn't want to go inside just yet.

"I didn't think you'd last long on the road with us," Rock said.

"Why not?"

"You've got a girl, and a life. I don't got shit, and you know me. The road is where I belong. Too much trouble happens when you stay in one place, believe me."

"I don't need to believe you. I lived in that shit. We met with The Skulls, and then got Devil's kid. Piston County felt like home, but I know that we fucked up at times settling down."

"Yeah, lot of shit went down. Lost some good people all over," Rock said.

"And I met the woman I was always going to have. I love her more than anything."

"I heard the tale of you and your woman. Doesn't it piss you off that you're here, and she's there?" Rock asked.

"Nope. You've got to know Lola to understand her reasoning. I don't have any regrets about what is happening." If he hadn't been with the Nomad Chapter, he wouldn't be here to help Lucius, and even though the other brother wouldn't admit it, Lucius was in so much fucking pain it was unreal.

"I didn't even know that Roxy was ill. What kind of sick shit is that? She seemed the same party animal I've come to know her as," Rock said.

"You didn't notice because you really didn't know her. When it's someone you love or someone you care about, you pay attention. It's the small things in life that you notice first. They seem unimportant to so many, but you know what they are, and you care."

"Wow, you sound like a man in love," Rock said. "Oh, that's right, pussy-whipped."

"Never said I wasn't pussy-whipped." Sinner

chuckled.

"I've never had that, you know?"

"Never had what?"

"A woman that you're willing to do anything for? To me, they've all been bitches. Holes that are available. No one has ever been something more."

Sinner shrugged. "Not all of them are the same. Lola, she's different. Not everyone's kind of girl, but she's mine." He laughed, thinking about her. "She's kind of a nerd actually. She's big with computers and stuff. I never understand what she's talking about, but to watch her on her computer, now that is enjoyable. We're two completely different people, and yet, we've found our way together."

"See, pussy-whipped."

"Why don't you criticize my feelings when you know what it's like." He slapped Rock on the back.

"Are you two done being pussies?" Lucius asked.

He glanced up at the other brother. "What's up?"

"Will you arrange your apartment? She doesn't have a lot of time left."

"Sure thing."

Lucius didn't linger. Sinner grabbed his cell phone and dialed Devil's number.

"This better be good, because you have woken Laurell up."

"Shit, sorry. Can you get my apartment ready?" Sinner asked.

"You and Lola coming home?"

"Nope. It's Lucius. He's going to need the club." Sinner explained what was happening, and at the end, Devil promised to have everything ready for when he needed it.

"Is Lucius okay?"

"I think this is going to hit him pretty hard,

Devil."

"We'll deal with it just like we've dealt with everything else."

Butler opened a window and began dusting everything down. Lola and Sinner didn't have a lot of crap to begin with. Devil had gotten a laundry company to come and cover the furniture with those plastic covers and stuff. He was removing them, as Jessica was cleaning out the bedroom. The club had rallied together to get the apartment ready for Sinner. Well, not Sinner, but Lucius and Roxy.

It had been a long time since Butler had seen Lucius. Too long. He was different now, off the drugs and hard partying.

The life Butler had now in Piston County, that was what had gotten him through. Each morning was a challenge. He reached for his coffee or water, never drugs. There had been times he would shoot up to start his morning.

No more.

He was all about clean living and shit. Angel had helped him with that. The drinks she made him and the recipes she gave helped him to find his inner peace.

Yeah, it was all just a bunch of bullshit, but it was what he enjoyed.

Natalie entered the apartment, and she was wearing her usual jeans and long shirt. She had stopped doing ranch work, and still she dressed each day as if she was.

She was so beautiful, so pure, and so…

"Can I talk to you?" she asked, coming toward him.

There was anger in her eyes, and she looked hurt.

"Sure, what is it?"

"Not here. Can we go somewhere quiet?"

He nodded and followed her out of the apartment. She was the one shining light in his life. He was older than she was, far more jaded, but she trusted him. She didn't know him when he was a druggie, an addict, a scumbag.

She was the first person to see him for him, and he loved her.

There. He finally said it. He loved her, and there was no other word for it. She meant everything to him, but the biggest problem was so did Slash, his brother.

They entered the steps leading down to the ground floor. She began to pace on the landing, and finally turned toward him.

"Why did you tell me about Slash?"

"I thought you'd like to know that he had feelings for you?"

"Why?" she asked. "Why couldn't you leave me in the dark? We were friends, and now I'm freaking out second guessing myself. I don't want him to think there is more going on, but I don't want to lose my friend. I don't have many of them."

Natalie had confided in him that she had struggled to make any kind of friends at school. There had been Paris, but because of her father's ranch, Natalie had been more boy then girl. So girls didn't want to be with her because she was too much of a boy. Boys didn't want to hang because she was a girl. So she was stuck for the most part on her own. It was where her art came in.

Butler would have loved to be with her, being in her company all day, every single day.

"I just thought you should know."

She paused, folded her arms, and glared at him. "What about you?"

"What about me?"

"Were you going to tell me how you felt as well?" she asked.

Butler paused. He should have known that Slash would tell her.

"I told you how much I valued your and Slash's friendship. Why did you have to spoil it, Butler? Why?"

"Because it's not a real friendship, is it?" he asked. "You think Slash is there just because he wants to be your friend, but it's not true. He's there because like everyone else in life, he wants something."

Tears filled her eyes. "Does that mean the only reason you've been nice to me is because you want something as well?"

"No, it's not."

"Well that is exactly what you just said. Thank you, Butler, thank you for putting me in my place." She left him in the stairwell, and he had completely fucked up.

He heard a door open, and there stood Slash.

"You come to fucking gloat?" Butler asked.

"Why the fuck would I gloat? You fucked us both over, and you think I'd party about that? What, rub it in your face?" Slash asked.

Butler sighed. "I would."

"I got to ask why, man? Why would you do it?"

"We both know it's not real what we're doing. We're her friend because we want her, simple as that."

Slash shook his head. "I was more than happy with just being her fucking friend, and now because you couldn't keep your fucking mouth shut, I'm not even going to have that. Thanks!"

Butler sighed. "I was trying to make it better."

"How is this making it better?"

"She has a right to know the truth. You want her because you want to fuck her."

Slash stepped up close to Butler. "Don't you fucking dare talk shit about her. You don't know me. You don't know my reasons."

"Come on, man, you think I don't know that you

want to slide inside her warm, wet, pussy? She's a virgin, you know. Never been touched by another man."

Butler expected the hit, and he got it. Slash slammed his fist into Butler's face. He didn't try to defend himself, and he took the hit, knowing he deserved it.

"You don't speak like that about her. I expect that kind of shit from Dick, but not from you."

Slash walked away, and Butler spat blood on the floor. It didn't feel good at all. In fact, he felt like the world's biggest asshole.

****

"Your apartment is nice. You really didn't need to go to this much trouble for me," Roxy said.

Sinner watched as she reached out to stroke a petal from some roses that Judi had picked up for him.

"It's fine."

"What about your girl?" Roxy asked.

"Don't worry about it."

Roxy's voice sounded weak, and she looked pale. She had some perspiration on her brow, and her hair looked lank.

She looked nothing like the woman he had met a couple of months ago. He couldn't even believe it had been a couple of months ago since he first met her. She had a way of making everyone feel part of her world.

"It's going to be interesting to see Lucius. He never fares well with being inside four walls for long."

"He didn't do too badly on our trip."

"Ah, did you notice that he made sure we kept on riding past some motels? He likes sleeping outside, something to do with looking up at the stars."

"How long have you known him?" Sinner asked, taking a seat beside her.

She held a pillow against her stomach. "All my

life. He was the bad boy growing up. The sinful guy, who turned into a ladies' man. We always got along. We met in the park, and he pushed the swing for me. He was so nice."

"He said you were in and out of hospitals."

"I was, but there were times I would get to be home. He wouldn't treat me like a freak, or like I was dying. He was nice to be around."

"He is angry right now," Sinner said, hating to point out the obvious.

"I know, and he's angry with me, and at my illness. He always was." She turned to smile at him. "Life is so damn short, Sinner. Really short. I envy people who are able to grow old, have everything within their grasp. I would love to have something like that, something to hold onto." She paused, and he saw the tear drip onto her chest. "I try to not let it get to me. I really do."

"Some days are tougher than others."

"Yeah, they really are."

There was a knock on the door, and Sinner went to answer it. He saw it was Devil, Ripper, and Judi.

"We thought we'd come and say hi," Judi said. "We came with chocolate."

"I like chocolate," Roxy said.

Sinner opened the door, and he waited for Roxy to give him a nod that she was fine. He needed some fresh air, and a smoke.

Once outside, the cold hit him hard, and he pulled his jacket up tight around him. He saw Lucius sitting on his bike with several cigarette butts around him.

"Is she settled?"

"Yeah, she is. Are you going up, or are you driving away?" he asked.

"I won't drive away," Lucius said.

"You've not been up to see her."

"I know." Lucius took a deep drag on his cigarette. "I've been here before you know. Not this town or anything, well, I've been here—what I mean is, I've done this with Roxy. Only she was younger, and we were both so young." He shook his head. "I didn't think she'd die then, but I know this is it. I go up there, and it's like I'm accepting that she's going to go." Lucius finished his cigarette stubbing it out.

"You love her?"

"She's my best friend, Sinner. She was the only person who didn't expect fucking shit from me. She didn't want me to be something for her. From the first moment I met her, we were just two people. I fucking hate this."

Sinner lit his own cigarette. "Why didn't you ever settle down with her?"

"We're friends, Sinner. I don't expect you to understand what I feel for her. We're the kind of friends that don't need to settle down and put meaning to it."

Lucius stared up at the apartment building, and he released a breath. "Fuck!"

"You're scared?"

"No. I'm not scared. Far from it. She's dying, Sinner. Roxy isn't going to see life past Halloween. I've got to live with that. I've brought her here to die because this is what she wants." Lucius stopped, and stared up at the building. He blew out a breath, and then headed toward the door.

"You know it doesn't make you less of a man admitting your feelings," Sinner said.

Lucius stopped to look at him. "I never denied my feelings, Sinner. I never needed to."

Sinner watched him make his way up to the apartment block, and all the time, he couldn't believe he was back home. Piston County was home.

It didn't take long for Devil, Ripper, and Judi to come down once Lucius went up.

"Well, he is as unfriendly as I remember," Devil said, coming toward him. "You okay?"

"I'm fine."

"She's one hell of a woman."

"You ever met her?" Sinner asked. "You know, before you came to see me?"

"I've seen Roxy before. You got to remember that I came to Piston County a while ago, and a lot has changed in that time. Lucius, he's gotten meaner. I could still kick his ass though."

Sinner laughed.

Devil had the respect of the club. He didn't need to kick anyone's ass.

"I wish I could say that there's going to be a feast at the clubhouse, but I can't," Devil said. "Lexie's bed-bound, and I don't want her stressing or over working herself."

"Okay. I didn't expect a big feast. This is home, and we're all friends here. I don't need my ass kissing."

"I wanted to ask you a favor, actually," Devil said.

"What?"

"Could you keep an eye on the kids and the club for me? I'm going to have a vasectomy."

"You're getting your balls chopped off?" Sinner asked.

"I'm done with the kids. We have enough, and Lexie's always sick through these pregnancies. The doctor has told us before that she won't get better, that she will in fact get worse as she gets older. I'm not going to risk her life for a kid."

"I'll take care of everything. I will."

"Thank you, Sinner. I appreciate it."

Devil slapped him on the back, and made to walk off.

"If I call Lola, can she help?"

"Of course," Devil said. "I didn't expect you to be able to handle everything. It's a fucking nightmare taking care of a wife and kids."

****

Two days later

"Lexie's been able to keep all of her food down," Lola said, putting the tray she had just carried down from the bedroom on the kitchen counter.

"We have one two boys and one girl ready for school. A little guy ready for playschool," Sinner said.

She turned to see the line of kids. They were handling this just fine. More than fine. "Why don't you guys go and watch some television while we wait for Phoebe to take you?"

"I can walk myself you know. I'm not a baby," Simon said.

"I know you're not, sweetie. There's so many dangers out there. We don't want Mommy stressing for nothing, do we?"

He shook his head. "Fine." He spun on his heel and off he went. She rolled her eyes, and went back to cleaning up the mess.

"I really do appreciate this," Sinner said.

"I told you I was more than happy to help out. Lexie is like my family as well." Lola had been thrilled to get his call for help.

"What about work? Were they happy to give you the time off?"

She wrapped up the bed, and looked at him, biting her lip. "Actually, I quit."

"What?"

"I quit work. I no longer wanted to do it, and when you called, I had already handed in my notice." She smiled at him. "I was heading back to Piston County."

"Oh. I had no idea."

"I'm not expecting anything. I know you've got to help Lucius and the club. I'm not rushing you or anything."

"I don't feel rushed." Sinner moved toward her, wrapping his arms around her. "Are you ready to come back home?"

"More than ready. I did what I needed to, and it's kind of strange, even though I hated it, I kind of loved it as well. I feel better. I feel like me." She wrapped her arms around his neck.

"You know, before you decided to have this break, you would never touch me outside of our apartment. Not even to hold my hand," he said.

"I didn't even notice."

"I'm a girl inside. I like the little things." He gave her a wink, and she laughed.

"You're a hoot."

He made an owl noise, and she loved it. She loved his playfulness that she had missed out on when they had been together before.

"How is Lucius handling everything?" She hadn't met the other brother yet. With Lexie's pregnancy she had stayed close, but now she was going to head over and see Roxy.

"He's … not. I don't know what he's doing to be honest. He's not his usual self, and I think it's killing him as much as it is her." Sinner pressed a kiss to her head. "I don't think I could bear anything like that happening to you."

"It has got to be tough."

The sound of a car honking had her pulling away. "That will be Phoebe. Let me get the kids."

She left the kitchen and herded the kids out toward Phoebe. She was in a family van, and even with all of her kids, there was enough room for Lexie's.

"You tell Lexie to take it easy, and I'll be by later, okay?" Phoebe asked.

"You got it. Take care."

Phoebe was Vincent's old lady. They had been in Piston County even before Chaos Bleeds had settled down.

Lola entered the kitchen to find Sinner wiping down a counter. Grabbing her bag, she moved toward him, wrapping her arms around him once again. "I'm going to head out. Is there anything you want?"

"Nope. I'm good. What are you going to get?"

"Some rolls for Lexie. She's craving some homemade soup. I'm going to drop in to see Roxy."

"Lola, I don't think that is a good idea."

"I want to meet her, Sinner. Let me."

He looked like he wanted to argue, and she kissed his lips.

She was at the door when he spoke.

"She's going to die, Lola. It's a guarantee. I don't want you getting to know her."

"Why?"

"When she dies, it'll hurt you. I can't have you hurting."

She took a deep breath. His concern was so damn sweet. "I know, but sometimes, we have to feel pain, Sinner. I want to know her. You've spoken so highly of her."

Without looking back, she made her way out toward her shitty car. Her belongings were in one of the spare rooms in Lexie's home. Sinner didn't share rooms with her at the moment. With the kids under Devil's roof, he had asked that they were discreet with any sex.

She wasn't about to disobey Devil's wishes.

The first stop she made was to the supermarket to get some general groceries. She had noticed that they were running out of milk, bread, cheese, and even pasta. Cooking for a large family was soon going to be impossible.

Lexie had warned her that if they tried to make boxed food then her kids would struggle to settle down for the night. Cooking from scratch it was, and Lola was okay with that.

She spent thirty minutes in the supermarket, before she was back in her car, and heading over to her and Sinner's apartment. She stopped when she saw a bike with a large, scary looking dude leaning against it. He was smoking, and looked freaked.

Don't be scared.

She grabbed her bag and climbed out. Instead of going straight to the apartment, she walked toward the biker.

"I'm not interested in a fuck. Move it along," he said.

"Are you Lucius?" She ignored his other comment.

"Who wants to know?" He certainly knew how to glare and look angry as fuck.

"I'm Lola." She held her hand out.

He stared at her hand, and then at her. "You're the girl that has been driving Sinner fucking crazy with all your bullshit."

She pulled her hand away.

"Yeah, you're here, aren't you?"

"I was just going to say it's nice to meet you."

"I wouldn't hold my breath for me to say the

same thing. Believe me, it's not likewise."

Gritting her teeth, she nodded. "I'm sorry." She turned away and made her way toward the door.

"Sinner's a good guy. Don't let him get away. He is fucking besotted with you."

She stopped long enough to hear him, and then vanished inside her apartment. Avoiding the elevator, she took the stairs, and by the time she got to her door, she was out of puff.

With a key in her hand, she was about to open the door, when she realized that Roxy had never seen her.

Knocking on the door, she heard some shuffling inside.

"Roxy, we've never met. I'm Lola. I belong to Sinner," she said.

The door opened, and the woman she saw took her by surprise. She had seen pictures on Sinner's cell phone. They were nothing like the woman before her.

For starters, the woman on the phone was full of life and love. This woman, she was really ill.

"Hey," Roxy said. "So, you're the mysterious Lola."

"And you're Roxy. I've met Lucius. Charming man."

Roxy laughed, and stopped, coughing. "Sinner didn't say anything about you being a joker."

"I'm not. Really, I'm not. I take everything too seriously. Lucius doesn't like me."

"At the moment, he doesn't like anyone. I wouldn't take it personally." Roxy took a seat on the sofa, and Lola sat opposite her in the chair. "He's hurting, and he doesn't know how to handle pain. Lucius lashes out at everyone when he's in pain. He's not happy with me."

"Was there any way you could treat this?" Lola

asked.

"No. The cancer had spread too fast. I could have prolonged my life, but I'd have been in a hospital all the time, having strange men poke and prod me. I'm not in the mood anymore to be poked by people I don't know. I wanted to live a little. You know?"

"I do. I get why you did what you did," Lola said. "He's going to miss you. Lucius."

"I know. I think that's my biggest regret. Not giving him time to come to terms with what is going to happen. He is used to me being well, you know. He doesn't want to admit that this is my end."

Lola stared at the woman, and she grieved for her.

"Is there anything I can do?"

"You could take care of Sinner. That man is a real special guy."

"I know." She had made one of the biggest mistakes of her life in walking away. Looking back, she knew deep in her heart that she had failed Sinner, and it was a miracle that he had loved her as much as he had. It hurt to know that she hadn't, at the time, loved him enough to fight for the two of them.

Everything she had done, she could have done *with* him, and with the club. Instead of seeing them as her family, she had just seen them as a crutch, a constant excuse not to take what she wanted.

Her love for Sinner had grown, and she couldn't lose him, not again. This was her fault, and she knew now what she had, and was thankful that he hadn't found anyone else. She was going to make sure that he didn't look elsewhere.

"No, I mean, seriously. I partied with that man, and not once did he look at another woman. He belongs to you so completely, and I'm not going to lie, I am totally jealous of you right now."

Lola smiled. "I love him, too. So much. I didn't love him right in the beginning. He deserves someone better than me, but I'm going to be better. I'm going to give him everything that he deserves in a woman."

"He told me what happened, just so you know. I needed to understand how a woman could let a man like Sinner go. After he explained everything, I saw that he got it. I get that you went through something awful, but you made a big mistake with Sinner. You gave him up, and all he ever did was love you. You can't go doing shit like that with someone that you love."

"I know. I wasn't good enough for him. I didn't want him to go through life afraid of something that would trigger a bad memory. Does that make me a bad person? I know it does. I shouldn't ask. I ... I was fucked up, and this is all my fault. I could have lost him."

"And you would have had no one to blame but yourself. Don't give him a chance to leave, Lola. Men like Sinner don't come around often, and they don't accept you treating them like crap, no matter how much you claim to love them."

"I know." She had messed up completely.

Roxy shook her head. "We do the craziest things for the people we love. Sinner stayed loyal to you, because he loved you. That's the crazy part. You left him, and he still loved you." She held onto a pillow, and Lola watched her. She looked so fragile. The illness was eating away at her. "That's all I'm going to say about it."

Silence fell between them, and Lola was reeling from everything that Roxy had said. The club, Lexie, Paris, they were all saying how supportive they were, but at the same time, she knew they were disappointed in her for leaving.

"Do you have any regrets?" she asked.

"I have loads. There are more than I can count.

My whole life has just been a bag of them." Suddenly Roxy looked so sad. "Life is so short, Lola. Don't waste a second of it. Please. I know you went to hell and back, but that's no reason to use as an excuse. Not anymore. Sinner loves you more than anything. Don't let him get away."

Lola felt tears spring to her eyes.

"You're so lucky to have a man that loves you."

"Lucius loves you."

"I know but not in the way that counts." Roxy reached out and caught her hand. There was no power to her grip, and it struck Lola that this woman was fading fast. "I'm so pleased I got the chance to see you."

Lola couldn't hold back. She closed the distance between them, and held the woman that had really struck her. It was merely a few minutes together, but it meant everything to Lola.

"Never give up, Lola. Hold on to what you've got."

She would. She would never allow herself to get lost again.

Chapter Thirteen

"Thank you so much for this, Sinner. I really do appreciate it," Lexie said.

He tucked in her blanket, and made sure her books were within reach. "You know the club adores you, and no one minds helping you out. You help with everyone at the club."

"I hate this. I love being involved, and right now I feel like a loser."

He chuckled. "Don't be."

"I've not met her, Sinner. I would love to have met her."

Sinner took her hand, giving it a squeeze. "You do not need to deal with what is going on."

"You're probably right. So, how are things with you and Lola?" Lexie asked.

"They're good. Do you know that she had quit her job?" He made sure her window was closed so that no cold air got into the room.

"Yes. I also know she has all of her stuff in the spare bedroom. I can't believe Devil has made you go home rather than be here."

"It's a good thing. We're still working through our problems, but I think we're almost there."

"You have issues?" Lexie asked, frowning.

"Not personal issues with each other, just problems that have caused us to separate."

He took a seat on the end of the bed as she patted it for him to. "When she first left, I was so damn angry with her," she said.

"Why?"

"She was giving up. At least it felt like it. She had been doing better, more than better, and yet, she was going to throw it all away. I know how good this club is. I know you've all done bad things. I get it, I understand it, all right? Some women, they really can't live with that knowledge, but I know how much Devil loves me and our children."

"I don't want you to hate Lola," he said. "She went through hell. You and I, we don't know what happened completely when she was taken by *him*. She was young. I'm a big man. I shouldn't have become so fucking miserable." He shrugged.

"You're both back now?"

"I'm not going anywhere." He looked around her room. "I've missed this place, and no, I don't mean your bedroom."

"You're not going to go back on the road?"

He shook his head. "No. I'm done. I think I've done what I really needed to do, you know? I was meant to be with Lucius, and help him through. Lola's back, and she's not going anywhere."

"Are you going to give her a reason to not leave?" Lexie asked.

"Of course. Now, you're going to rest, and we're going to deal with this, okay."

"Yes." Lexie flumped back. "Oh, there has been a change of plans for Christmas as well. Because I can't go anywhere or do anything, some of The Skulls are coming here. I believe Angel, Lash, and her kids are coming. She'll be making dinner, obviously."

"Don't you worry about a thing. All you'll be allowed to do is sit and look pretty."

"Rude."

"You know you love it." He left the room, whistling as he went. The house was clean completely, and he was rather pleased with his ability to find order around chaos. With a bunch of kids running around, he was surprised to see it was kind of clean.

He found Devil in the kitchen.

"Are you heading to the hospital?" Sinner asked.

"Yes. Vincent is outside waiting for me."

"Are you sure you don't want any of the brothers with you?"

"Vincent's part of the club. You know that. I'm going to go and see her. How is she?"

"I think she's looking better to be honest, much, much better."

"I don't want her stressing." Devil left him alone, and Sinner took the time to make himself a drink.

This was crazy what was happening.

Humming to himself, twenty minutes passed before Devil came down. He had a smile on his face.

"I take it that conversation went well."

"Being with my woman makes me smile. She doesn't want me to have the procedure, but every time we're pregnant, she doesn't want to be in bed all the time. So, away I go. Take care of them for me."

"Of course. You know you can count on me."

****

"It's about time that you remembered me," Paris said.

Lola opened her arms. "Can I have a hug?"

Paris had Aria in her arms, and she changed her to one hip, and then pulled Lola in close. "Of course. I've missed you so much. I had to hear everything from Lacey. Why did you stop calling me?" she asked.

"I don't know. It just didn't feel right to be calling anyone. I stopped calling Lexie as well."

"Are you here to stay or just for a visit?" Paris asked.

Lola took Aria from Paris as they entered the kitchen. "Wow, you've grown so big so quickly."

"Yes, she has. She's been a total blessing though." Paris smiled at her daughter, and Lola saw all the love in her eyes. "You didn't answer my question."

"I'm here to stay. I'm not going anywhere anymore."

"Did you meet a handsome man on your travels?" Paris asked.

"I didn't do much traveling. When I went out with Sarah and Belinda—they were friends I met at work—there were some guys, but I wasn't interested to be honest. I never left Sinner. Not in my heart, I love him. I do."

"You left so quickly."

"I felt I had to. You know. You were able to deal with everything so quickly and swiftly. I thought I was the same, but I wasn't."

Paris shrugged. "We're different. I know Sinner was never the same without you. Spider, he was worried about him all the time. You took a big part of Sinner when you left."

"I'm back, and Sinner's back. We're not going anywhere." She kissed Aria's head.

"Have you talked to your parents?" Paris asked.

"Not you as well?"

Paris held up her hands. "I come in peace, and all that. They call me from time to time to ask about you. From what they tell me, you don't talk to them, not one bit."

Lola sighed. "It was easier that way."

"They're still your parents. They love you."

"They were always looking at me as if I was fragile. I hated it." She stared into Aria's eyes, at the innocence of her. Lola was overcome by how protective she was of the little girl.

"I would kill anyone who would harm her," Paris

said. "Sometimes I've thought about what would have happened if it had been Aria and not me, and I get so angry. She's my little girl. My life, my everything. I love her so much."

Lola released a breath, trying to stop herself from crying. "I promised myself I wouldn't cry."

"The point is, Lola, that you're someone's little girl. Spider, he would destroy everyone in his path because he has the power to do it. Some parents, they don't have that ability. They cannot kill without blinking, and they don't have a club to help them through. Your parents were all alone. They were scared to death that they would lose you. Not only that, as a parent you want the best for your kid. Whenever your father looked at you, he knew he had failed, honey. How do you think that made him feel?"

Lola hadn't given her father a single thought. Biting her lip, she stared at her friend, and shook her head. "I screwed up, didn't I?"

"Yeah, you did. You need to give them a chance, honey. They're your parents. They love you more than anything else in the world. I know I wouldn't want anything to happen to Aria. It would kill me, but I tell you what, I would hunt the bastards down, and I would destroy them." Paris finished making a drink. "Have a seat and tell me about everything."

Lola didn't know what to say. Paris had just opened her eyes, and when she looked at Aria, she saw her own child. What would she have been like if what happened to her ever happened to one of her kids? She would be in complete pain and chaos. She would want to kill the people herself with her bare hands.

Lola didn't stay long with Paris, just long enough to catch up, and then she was back in her car, and headed toward Lexie's house. Sinner was there, and they swapped places. She kissed him, and he pressed her against the wall, promising to be back later. Her stomach had butterflies with the passion in his voice and the way he looked at her.

Lexie was reading, and after delivering her some soup and bread for lunch, Lola was alone. Since being back, she had taken the responsibility of being in charge of the website, much to Natalie's relief.

Modifying the website, she made the necessary changes and updated it. Once that was done, she simply stared at her computer and her cell phone.

If she called now, they would be home. She knew this.

Stop being a baby.

Releasing a breath, she picked up her cell phone, and tapped on the screen bringing up her parents' home number. It would be so easy to call them. Just a couple of clicks and she would be dialing.

"She's my little girl. My life, my everything. I love her so much."

She had been her father's little girl, and her mother had loved her even when she loved computers more than she loved dressing up in girl's clothing.

Finally, she dialed her parents' number, pressing the cell phone to her ear. She couldn't stop the tears from falling, nor could she stop the sudden fear that maybe she had left it too long, and she had. She avoided everything with them.

"Hello," her father said, and she froze.

Seconds passed.

"Hello, is there anyone there?"

She gritted her teeth. The desire to put the phone down and ignore it was strong, but she fought it. "Hey, Dad," she said.

"Lola?"

"Yeah, it's me."

"Honey, come quick, it's Lola." She heard him shout.

"How have you been?" she asked.

"Me, I've been fine. What about you? How have you been?"

"I've been doing okay. I left Piston County for a little while, and I got a different job. I'm back now. I was just so bored." Whizz's offer had been too good to turn down. Her life wasn't away from the club anymore. It was part of it.

"It's so good to hear your voice." This was from her mother.

"Hey, Mom. How are you?"

"I'm over the moon that you've decided to call."

Guilt gripped her, and she deserved it. "I'm sorry. I really am. I had a lot of things on my mind, and I took it out on you guys. I really shouldn't have."

"Honey, we would do anything for you. We love you so much," her father said.

"I love you, too. It's, I'm so sorry. I suck at this so much." She laughed. "I'm a little busy at the moment. I'm helping out one of the girls, Lexie. She's having a few problems with her pregnancy, but I was wondering if you would like to go for a visit."

"We would love you to, honey. We really would."

"Would you like to meet Sinner? I know you didn't want me dating, Dad, but I love him, and he is part of my life."

"You love him?" her father asked.

"Yeah, more than anything. He's my soul mate."

"Of course, we would love to see him. You and him both."

She nodded. After talking a little more and

catching up, she finally put the phone down.

"We're heading out to see your parents?" Sinner asked, making her jump.

"Geez, you scared me," she said. "I thought you were on your way to Naked Fantasies."

"I was, and well done. You said it without a sneer."

"I don't like the thought of any naked woman throwing themselves at you. Sue me."

He laughed. "There is no naked woman, and besides, the only one I want is you." He moved close, and kissed her lips. "You want me to go and see your family?"

"Of course." She took his hand, locking their fingers together. "We're in this together now, right? Forever?"

"Yeah, we really are." He pressed a kiss to her lips. "I wish you could come with me."

"I need to be here for Lexie. I will get started on some food for when the kids get home. How does chicken noodle soup sound?"

"Sounds awesome. I love noodle soup." He pressed a kiss to her lips, and she watched him walk away, heading toward the club's titty bar. She didn't like Naked Fantasies, but she trusted Sinner. He would never step out on her.

****

Devil was back within three days, but Lola and Sinner still stayed at their place. Lexie told Sinner that he could sleep in Lola's room, and he didn't have to keep going back to the club. Of course, Devil wanted to argue, but Lexie had the last word in everything, not that he minded.

Lexie was damn good for the club, and she reminded Devil that they were older than a couple of high school kids.

Roxy had deteriorated and was refusing to see a doctor. Jessica went to visit her, and warned them all to be prepared, that it wasn't good news at all.

Everyone was waiting for that call of doom, and around it, Sinner was in fucking heaven. He wanted to feel guilty about his newfound happiness, but he couldn't. Lola, she had found whatever it was she needed, and now he didn't feel like he was the only one that wanted to be a couple. Every step of the way, she was there, she was making decisions, and she was even initiating sex, which was fantastic. It was like the past Lola had been nothing more than a shell. Living her life without really being passionate about anything. Looking back, Sinner finally realized that he'd not had Lola then. No, she wasn't with him. Now, she *was* with him, and their relationship had gotten stronger for their period away from each other.

Late one night after making love to Lola, he turned her to face him.

"What's the matter?" she asked.

"I don't want us to ever regret a moment of being together," he said.

"I don't."

He pressed a kiss to her lips, and stared into her eyes.

"This is about Roxy?" she asked.

He nodded.

"She told me to never have any regrets. She doesn't want me to live thinking about tomorrow, but to live in the now. I'm going to take her advice about that."

He held onto her hand, and ran his thumb across the finger that would hold his ring if they ever got married.

"Marry me, Lola?" he asked.

"Sinner?"

"No, I'm being real right now. I want to marry you. I want to spend the rest of my life with you. I don't give a shit about everything else. Yes, I sometimes leave the toilet seat up, and you leave your towel on the floor. We share a toothbrush at times. None of that matters. We've wasted so much time already. I don't want to waste anymore. I love you, only you."

She cupped his face, and he waited. "Yes. I'll marry you. There is no one else that I would want." She pressed her lips against his, and they moaned. He wrapped his arms around her, holding her close, and knowing in his heart he never wanted to let go.

****

Lucius finished reading the trashy romance book and could just about vomit. This was what women were reading nowadays. Men were not fucking like that, and if they were, he was surrounded by a bunch of pussies.

There was a knock at the door, and he frowned seeing as it was quite late.

Heading toward the door, he opened it up to see the frumpy woman in boys' clothing. Her hair was in two ponytails, each one trailing down her breasts. She was curvy, and pretty in the girl next door way.

She was also smiling at him. "Hey, I'm Natalie."

"Hello, Natalie. Sorry to bother you and all, but Roxy asked for me to bring you this." She handed him over a thermos.

"Why the fuck would she want you to do that?"

"It's from her recipe. I was here earlier today when you were out for a smoke. She asked for a favor, and I'm not one to turn down an opportunity to give."

He took the thermos, and she stepped away.

Nodding his head, he thanked her, and watched as she left. Not once did she try to get on her knees to suck his cock.

Closing the door, he made his way into the bedroom. Roxy was lying on the bed, resting her head on a pillow, her eyes open.

"Why?" he asked.

"You never eat properly when you're upset, and I know how you like your food."

"Are you trying to matchmake?" he asked, not interested in the frumpy girl.

Roxy shook her head. "No. She's got her hands full with two men here."

"She fucking two men? She didn't seem the sort to be that kinky."

"Not two men at once, you big oaf. Two men who want her."

"Who?"

"I think those romance books have gone to your head."

"Have you read them?" Lucius said. "Yuck."

"Yeah, yeah, yeah. I bet you got a couple tips. I know you, Lucius, you'd do anything to make you the best lover in the whole world."

"So, you still didn't tell me who?" he asked.

"Fine. It's Slash and Butler. They both like her, and they have both hurt her because she's not like other women. She doesn't understand them one bit."

He opened up the thermos and took a deep inhale of the liquid. "This is so good. Thank you."

"I'm always looking after you." Roxy sighed. "Tell me you'll be okay."

"Let's not do this, okay? You do not have to worry about me at all. I'll be fine. You know this, and you know me."

She gave him that sad smile, and he forced the pain aside. This wasn't about him. This was about her.

****

Natalie wrapped her jacket around her as she stepped out into the cold. Roxy had asked her to make the soup that had a little hint of spice. It was something that always brought Lucius comfort, and right now, he needed it.

She closed her eyes, feeling the loss of this woman that she had known for a handful of hours. Life was cruel. It was unfair.

"You okay, pet?" Slash asked. She would recognize his voice.

Opening her eyes, she saw Slash near one bike, and turning her head, she saw Butler next to the other. This was not happening. She wouldn't get drawn into this game.

"I'm fine," she said. Butler was near the front of her car, while Slash was near the back. She hated this. "I came to drop off some soup. Are you guys following me now?"

"We wanted to make sure you're all right, and I wanted to apologize," Butler said. "I shouldn't have told you about Slash."

"And I shouldn't have told you about Butler."

"It doesn't change anything," she said, looking between the two of them. "I appreciate that you came with me, honestly, I do, but I can't do this. I don't know what you expect of me. I'm not used to this. I don't want to be caught in the middle with either of you, and I don't want to have to choose either. I care for you both." Why did it have to be complicated like this?

"What if you gave us both a chance to win you?" Slash asked.

"It's not a competition, not even close. I just want to go home now." She went to her car, and without looking at either of them, she drove away.

Chapter Fourteen

Roxy died a week later. No one knew what happened, only that Lucius was with her. Sinner didn't think he would shed a tear for a woman he barely knew, but he did. Roxy, in her charming way, had touched the lives of them all in a short time.

For funeral arrangements, they found a plot in Piston County, and they all paid in to make sure she could have a proper burial. Roxy had been sure to make her own arrangements, and had given them to Lucius.

She didn't want anyone but the Chaos Bleeds crew there.

Standing by her graveside in the freezing cold, Sinner held onto Lola as his woman cried. Lexie was out as well. She refused to be left in bed when a woman she hadn't known but heard wonderful things about had been laid to rest.

Lucius, he didn't cry. He stood by Roxy's graveside with a single white rose. He looked as cold as stone.

Everyone was here, the Chaos Bleeds crew, and several of the Nomad Chapter, including Rock and Crow. Seeing Crow was a shock. He looked vicious, deadly, scary.

"Would you like to say a few words?" the priest asked.

Lucius stared at the gravestone, and nodded.

Sinner tensed up, waiting. The anger inside Lucius eyes couldn't be mistaken. He was livid, and right now, he was a dangerous man.

"Roxy was … she was a firecracker." He laughed. "Wherever she went, she would light up a room no matter what. She had been sick for a long time, and she has spent most of her life going in and out of hospitals. All she ever wanted to do was bring happiness to this world, to let everyone know that it is better to love than it is to hate." Lucius stopped and paused.

Lola grabbed Sinner's hand, holding him.

"When I look around right now, I know she touched each and every one of you. Thank you so much for your support these past couple of weeks. Thank you for being there. Roxy would have loved to have seen this outcome. She always said she would see more people in death than in life."

They smiled.

"Love you, Roxy girl, love you, and I'm going to miss you." Lucius placed the rose on her coffin, and stepped back. Lola released Sinner, and added hers. Everyone from Chaos Bleeds put a rose on top of Lucius's.

They all stayed to pay their respects, and when it was over, Sinner watched as Lucius was the first to leave. He climbed on his bike, and headed in the direction of the clubhouse.

"We're having a small get-together," Devil said, coming toward them. "You're free to come to the clubhouse."

Sinner nodded.

"Are we going?" Lola asked.

"I think it's best. I want to keep an eye on Lucius."

"You think he's going to cause trouble?"

"I think right now he's hurting, and Lucius could do anything."

Lola drove in her shitty car, which he was determined to have changed once life got back to some semblance of normality. They were both living with Devil and Lexie, which felt like being under Mom and

Dad's roof. He didn't mind so much, but waking up to find Devil's ugly ass in the bathroom was not a pretty sight. The bedroom they were sharing didn't have an en suite, and when he asked Devil about it, he was told that Devil wasn't about to waste money on bathrooms that would rarely be used.

Pulling up at the clubhouse, he saw that several couples had arrived.

"I don't think Lexie should be here," Lola said.

"Devil's made sure that Jessica stays with her." They entered the clubhouse, and he found Lucius at the bar. None of them were wearing their leather jackets. They had decided to see Roxy off in the formal style, and even Lucius was wearing a suit.

Sinner watched as Lucius downed three scotches within a matter of minutes. Nothing was happening, so he took a seat with Paris, Spider, Death, and Brianna.

"It's okay, honey," Death said, stroking Brianna's hair.

"If it's okay, why do you keep staring at him?" she asked.

"I'm just making sure everything is okay."

Death and Spider nodded at him. They all knew of Lucius's reputation. He could be fine one moment, and lash out the next. He didn't mind. Most of the times when Lucius lost his temper, it was with people who deserved it. At Chaos Bleeds clubhouse, they had their women, and right now, all of the brothers sensed Lucius's pain, his anger, his rage.

"If anything happens, I want you to go, okay?" Spider said.

"This is kind of scaring me," Paris said. "You guys are not going to fight each other. We're remembering Roxy here."

"I know, but you don't get it. This can get ugly

really fucking fast."

****

Lucius knew they were worried. All of the brothers were watching him, waiting for him to snap. He was fine with it. They didn't know him, not really. The only woman who ever knew him was dead, six feet fucking under now, and there wasn't a damn thing he could do about it.

Roxy was gone, and none of them even knew a thing about her, not really.

The tears were not going to fall. He didn't want to sit and wallow. He wanted to hurt someone or something.

Taking the glass of scotch, he swallowed it down in one gulp. He didn't even get any of the burn. Right now, he just wanted oblivion, and he wanted pain. They were the two emotions he could deal with. Everything else could fade the fuck away so long as he had that.

"Hey," Natalie said. She was the girl that gave him the thermos a week ago. She smiled at him, but it didn't reach her eyes. She was hurting as well. Everywhere he looked people were hurting. That was how good Roxy was.

She gave and gave.

"Roxy wanted me to give this to you. She told me to wait until after her funeral." She handed him a book. It was a small leather-bound book. He had seen Roxy working on it for years, and had been scribbling away at it the past couple of months.

"Thank you."

"I am really sorry for your loss. I know we've only known her a short time, but you knew her for longer." She crossed her arms.

Out of the corner of his eye, he saw Butler and Slash move a little closer. They were concerned for Natalie, and they both wanted her. He stared at her, and he knew exactly how to get what he wanted.

Reaching out, he stroked a finger down her cheek, and then grabbing her arms, he pulled her close. "I wonder how they will handle this."

Before anyone could stop him, he slammed his lips down on Natalie's. She didn't fight him to start, and he was pleased about that. He was many things, but a rapist wasn't one of them. The moment Natalie started to fight, he released her. She was shocked and embarrassed. Within seconds, Butler was there, grabbing him.

Spinning around, Lucius landed his first blow to Butler, and that was when the fighting really started. This was what he needed, what he craved. The violence was what had to happen. He couldn't live without it, and wouldn't want to.

Landing blow after blow, Slash and Butler came at him. Next, Death was there, and Rock grabbed him with Crow, and they tried to hold him down.

"You need to stop."

He shook his head. Roxy was gone. He knew what he needed, and it wasn't to be forced aside.

Jerking the two men, he made them collide together. Lucius was known for never backing down, and for always finishing what he started.

There was only one man he had never taken down, and right now, Devil was in front of him. The women had left the clubhouse, and there were several tables shattered on the floor.

"You think this is the way?" Devil asked.

"You got a problem with me, Devil?"

"No, I don't have a problem with you, Lucius." Devil removed his jacket, and rolled up his sleeves. "We both know what you want. Why didn't you just ask for it? Roxy is gone. She is never coming back. You think she will want this?"

This was what he needed. Charging at Devil, he landed a blow to his side, but Devil had already swung, landing three blows in succession to Lucius's head. When that didn't help, Lucius grabbed Devil around the waist, going to lift him up. Devil kicked his knee up, getting Lucius's balls.

Each strike of pain felt good to him. It was what he wanted, what he needed, and what he reveled in.

The pain.

It would stop him from hurting, from fucking feeling this pain that wouldn't go away, nor would it die.

Devil grabbed his head, and slammed it against the side of wall.

Lucius went down, dazed.

"I get it," Devil said. "You're hurting, and you wanted someone to help deal with that pain. Nothing is going to help, and I refuse to beat the shit out of you every single day until you can handle it. I'm sorry about Roxy, I really am, but you cannot take this shit out on my club. I won't let you do that." Devil knelt down. "The club is here for you, brother. Every single one of us is here for you. I know you're in pain right now. And I'm sorry about that."

Lucius stared up at the ceiling, and he hated this feeling. "I've got to go."

"You don't have to leave. There is a room for you here whenever you need it."

He shook his head, and stood up. "No. I've got to go." Lucius grabbed the leather-bound book, and made his way out of the clubhouse. There were several men and women, whom he ignored. Climbing onto his bike, he pulled out of the clubhouse without looking back. His time in Piston County was over, and there was no way in hell he was coming back.

****

"I'm fine," Devil said.

"He hit you," Lexie said. "I should kick his ass."

"He was too big for you, Mom," Simon said. "You wouldn't have been able to kick anything." Simon continued to much on his cereal as Lexie poked his head. It didn't hurt at all, but it was good to have his woman in his arms. "Can I buy Tabby a present?"

"What for?" Devil asked. He tried not to wince as she used an anti-bacterial wipe on his cut. Lucius was a mean ass motherfucker. Whenever they had been on the roads, and Lucius got into one of these moods, Devil had been the one to calm him down, simply because he made him stay down.

"For Christmas. She likes to write like everything down. She keeps these journals and stuff. Can I get her something like that?"

Lexie smiled at him. He rolled his eyes.

"Why don't you get her a doll or something?"

"Dad, this is Tabby. Not everyone wants a doll."

"It's Tabby, Daddy," Lexie said. "She's special, and she writes and everything."

"Mommy, that's not fair," Simon said.

Lexie giggled. "I'm only kidding, son." She kissed Simon's head, and padded over to the stove. Devil was on his feet, and picking her up. "Stop that, I weigh a ton."

"You're light as a feather, babe. Come on, time to put you to bed. You've had enough excitement for one day." He carried her upstairs, passing Lola and Sinner's room as they did. Devil paused as he heard the sound of feminine moaning, and Lexie giggled. "This is why I didn't want them sharing a room."

"Come on, they're back together again, and that's a good thing."

"I don't care. You heard Simon."

"He's not about to start sleeping with Tabitha. He's a boy that wants to get her a journal, not expensive lingerie. I'd start worrying when he asks to get her underwear," she said, kissing his neck. "You need to learn to relax a little."

"I can't help it. All I fear is I'm going to have a bunch of little Simons and Tabithas running around the house."

"So?"

"I'm too young to be a granddad."

"You better get used to it. They are going to make us grandparents before you know it." She pressed her lips against his, silencing any other protest from him.

Devil was going to make sure that the moment Simon was even close to thinking about sex, he was going to be having that birds and bees talk.

Chapter Fifteen

"You don't have to pretend to be someone else," Lola said. "I'm happy with you going in your jacket."

"I've nearly done," Natalie said.

Sinner glanced over to see Natalie finishing with his patch. She had removed the Nomad Chapter, and was now finishing with the Piston County patch that Devil had everyone include on their jacket.

"I don't want to embarrass you," he said. "This is a big deal."

"We're going to see my parents, who already know that you're part of a biker club. It's not a conspiracy," she said.

Devil was at the stove, frying up some eggs and bacon while the kids were in front of the television. "Will you two be back for dinner?" he asked.

"Nope," Lola said. "I've done you guys some chicken salsa. It's in the fridge, and I've given you instructions on how to heat it up. You'll be fine."

"What about the kids?"

"It's not spicy, and there is a jar of hot sauce if you need to add a little more kick to it." Lola finished washing the dishes.

"Are you staying for dinner?" Devil asked, looking at Natalie.

"Nope. I'm just here to let Lexie look over some sketches, and I'm also doing this for him." She pointed at Sinner.

"You cannot sew?" Devil asked.

"I can."

Natalie snorted.

"Not very well."

"Butler's arranged for your apartment to be

cleaned." Devil handed him back the keys. "When you're ready to move in, you can."

"What about a nanny?" Lola asked. "We were helping you out."

"I'm the new nanny," Natalie said. "I'm going to be taking your old room. I hope that is okay."

"You're kicking us out?" Sinner asked.

"I'm politely asking you to leave, and I appreciate all the help. I know Natalie won't have any funny business going on inside her room, and with Simon, let's just say I want less influence."

"Seriously? You and Lexie were constantly at it."

"And this is my house. I know what I want, and the two of you are going to see that I get it." Devil gave them a wink. "Enjoy your stay with your parents." He left to deliver Lexie her breakfast.

"How come you didn't tell me?" Lola asked, looking at Natalie.

"I thought you would be thrilled. You don't have to keep your voice down, and you were saying the other day in the shop how hard it is to not scream and beg for more."

Lola's face went beet red. Sinner chuckled, and Natalie just kept on working.

"What's going on with you, Butler, and Slash?" he asked.

"Nothing. I don't know why people are so afraid of bikers. You're all just a bunch of gossipers. It's not funny at all. You're always into everyone's business."

"I'm sure you're charmed by us really," he said.

She rolled her eyes. "Totally. There you go, all done." She held his jacket out to him. "Next time, don't try and do this yourself. You can ruin the leather if you're not careful."

He took the jacket from her, thanking her.

Lola grabbed her bag, and together they made their way outside. He went to her shitty ass car, and Lola stood by his bike. She wore a pair of jeans and shirt. To him, she looked sexy as he got to see the full roundness of her juicy ass.

"We're not going in your car?" he asked.

"Nope. I thought we could ride to my parents' place. It could be fun." It would explain why her bag was in fact a backpack, which she put on her shoulders, tightening it up.

She held out his keys for him to take. "Take me for a ride, bad boy."

He laughed. Straddling his bike, he waited for her to climb on after him, and then gave her the helmet.

"No. Come on."

"You didn't want to come on my bike before. I'm a big believer in safety first."

"You're a pain in the ass," she said, taking the helmet from him, and putting it right on her head. "I hate this."

"Safety first."

When she had her arms wrapped around him, he pulled away from Devil's home, and onto the main road. She held him tightly as he maneuvered the roads, and he was so full of fucking pride. Finally, Lola was on the back of his bike, and he was so happy. Nothing would take away from this moment.

He was nervous about meeting her parents, but he would do anything for his woman.

The ride took a couple of hours, and even though it was cold, Lola didn't complain. By the time they pulled up outside of her childhood home, Sinner felt the girl that had been taken by Andrew. Lola had a loving family, and had the parents that loved her, life that meant nothing bad was ever going to happen, and yet, it had.

She hadn't been able to get away from what happened to her.

Lola climbed off the bike and passed him the helmet. She shook her hair out, groaning. "That thing is like death." She pressed her hands to her face, and squished. "I feel like my face looks like that." She moved her lips, looking like a fish, and he laughed.

"You are a real goofball."

He climbed off the bike, and Lola took his hand. They turned toward her house just as the front door opened up.

A woman that was in her late fifties stood in the doorway. She looked a little like Lola, and behind her was a big man.

"This is it," Lola said.

She held onto his hand, and together they entered her home. He saw her father assessing him, glaring, and looking like he wanted to kill him. Sinner was used to being thought of as the enemy, so he did his best to smile, and do his part.

They were invited in, and Sinner stood back as they embraced her.

"Mom, Dad, I would like you to meet Sinner. He's my fiancé."

"I don't see a ring on your finger," her dad said.

"I know. We haven't gotten around to getting a ring yet. I don't mind."

Sinner shook her dad's hand. The old man squeezed, and Sinner didn't blink an eye, squeezing right back.

"Why don't you boys go and talk, and I'll take Lola to help me get drinks ready?"

"Sounds fantastic."

They entered a sitting room, and Sinner saw there were lots of pictures of Lola growing up. In the corner by the television, he saw one of her next to a computer that had a ribbon wrapped around it.

"So, are you responsible for keeping Lola away from us?" her dad asked.

Sinner smirked. "No. We both know that was Lola's decision, not mine."

"You could have encouraged her to come back home."

Sinner sat down in the chair opposite her father. "You want to blame me for shit I had no control of, fine. I really don't care. You don't like me, again I could care less. I'm here because Lola asked me to be here, no other reason. You got me. I love your daughter, and if you think for a second that you're going to push me away because you don't think I'm good enough, you're wrong." Sinner wasn't about to be pushed around.

"I want my little girl."

"And she's right here. If you must know, you and your wife pushed her away. She couldn't deal with how you treated her. After everything that happened, she found it impossible to handle you. You always looked at her like a victim, like you had to be scared in case she went off the rails."

"You think you did any better?" he asked.

Sinner shook his head. "Nope. I messed this up as well. We took a break recently. Both of us had some time away. Lola wanted it, I didn't, but I did it for her. She needed it, and everything that has happened has been because of Lola. She's a strong woman, your daughter. She won't break. You've got to give her a chance here." He would not have her upset.

"Do you really love my daughter?"

"More than anything in the world. I would do anything for her, and I have. Do you think it easy for me to let her go? It wasn't. Every single fucking day it was a fight to not go after her. Letting her go, it was the hardest thing I have ever done, and believe me when I say I have done a lot in my time. Never once have I felt tested the way I did with Lola. I love her more than anything. There is not a man out there who would replace me. I would die for her." Walking away when he went to see her, going back with the Nomad Chapter, he had done it so that he didn't go get Lola, and force her back. The temptation had always been there, but he had known deep down into his soul that she had to be away from him. She had to grow, and by letting her go, they had both found their way back together.

"Are you both still alive in there?" Lola asked.

"We're fine, honey. You can come in."

Sinner smiled as she entered the room, carrying a tray of drinks. She looked so damn nervous, and he was determined not to spoil this for her. She handed out the drinks, and took a seat on the arm of the chair beside him. When she reached for his hand, he took it, locking their fingers together.

"Are you two pregnant?" her father asked.

"Dad!"

"Not yet, sir, but one day, I'm hoping we have some good news like that."

****

Later that night, back home at Lexie and Devil's house, Lola put the last of the boxes on the floor. They only had a few items in the spare bedroom. She tucked some of her hair behind her ear, and glanced around the small room.

"What are you thinking about over there?" Sinner asked, entering the room. He had a towel wrapped around his waist. He sat down on the bed, staring at her.

"I don't know. I think we're starting a new chapter of our life together, you know? It's kind of scary."

"You're afraid?"

"No. I'm excited. I don't know what the future holds, but it's something to look forward to." She took his hand. "I heard what you said to my dad."

"I meant every word."

"Did you really want to come and get me?" she asked.

"Yeah, I did. Every single day I wanted to come to you and drag you back home."

"What stopped you?" She stared into his eyes, knowing that if he had come for her, she would have gone willingly. Would she have been where she was now? Probably not. She would have still been trapped in the same nightmare that she wouldn't have been able to escape from.

"I realized that if I came and got you, and forced you back, that's not how I wanted us to be, Lola. I wanted us to be together like Lexie and Devil, Ripper and Judi, even Dick and Martha. I wanted us to be together because it was what we both wanted more than anything. I loved you enough to let you go." He pressed a kiss to her head, and she smiled.

"You have always been so good to me. Too good." She squeezed his hand, not wanting to let him go.

"We both did what we needed to do."

She thought about his Nomad Chapter patch, which then made her think of Lucius. "Have you heard from Lucius?"

Sinner shook his head. "Rock has tailed him. If he gets into trouble, the club has eyes on him, but right now, he's working off his pain."

"He works off his pain?" she asked.

"He always has. Aggression, anger, it was what Lucius has always been known for. Makes no sense as to what Roxy saw in him."

"What did you think happened that last night?" she asked.

"I don't know. Roxy was fading fast, and the medicine wasn't doing anything to help the pain."

"What's going on in that head of yours?" She could tell when there was more he wanted to say. Sinner pulled her into his lap.

"Roxy and Lucius had a strange friendship. They both cared about each other, and loved each other, in their own ways."

"We both know this."

"Yes. I think Lucius took Roxy's pain away, which was why he was so angry. He was angry at himself for giving in."

"He killed her?"

He shook his head. "No. He took her pain away. Think about it, babe. She was hurting."

Tears filled Lola's eyes. She felt such utter sadness for Roxy and for Lucius.

"He needs to do what he needs to do. He's a stronger man than I am."

"Why?"

"I couldn't live without you, babe. Wouldn't want to." He pressed a kiss to her lips, and he moved her to the bed so that she was flat on her back.

She gasped as he pressed a kiss to her breast. The shirt she wore did nothing to cover the fact she wasn't wearing a bra. Through the fabric of her shirt, he sucked on her nipple, making her moan and arch up against him.

"You're so beautiful," he said.

Suddenly, he pulled away, and she watched, a little annoyed that he had stopped, when he reached for something. Seconds later, she saw what it was. A gold band. "I did go out and buy you a ring. I didn't know when the best time would be to give it to you."

"And right now when you're about to fuck me, you thought was the best time?"

"I really do love your sexy mouth." He took her bottom lip, biting it. Pulling up, he held her hand, and slid the band onto her finger. It fit perfectly.

"We're going to have to start making preparations now," she said. "Do you think we should wait until after Lexie gives birth? She loves helping with these sorts of things."

"I think it's the least we could do."

He bent down, and claimed her lips. Grabbing her hands, he pressed them to the bed. His cock was rock hard, pressing against her stomach.

Lola opened up to him, and he took, making love to her in every way that he could, and she knew it was going to be a future to remember. This man was indeed her soul mate, the love of her life.

****

Butler drank his sweet fruit drink and tried to ignore the man across the room, playing pool. He hadn't spoken to Slash in weeks, ever since Natalie had pretty much told them no.

"You're going to have to talk to him," Martha said, taking a seat beside him. Dick was beside his woman, giving him the stink eye, and letting him know if he said some nasty shit to her, they would be outside fighting it out.

"I'm not talking to him."

"You're being a baby," Martha said.

"I don't blame Natalie for turning them both down. They're being pricks," Dick said.

"Fuck you," Butler said.

"Then go and talk to Slash, and stop being a fucking girl."

Martha slapped Dick's chest. "Remember, we're not judging."

"I'm not judging them. I'm just stating a fact. They're being pussies over this woman. No wonder she decided to be Devil's nanny. She knows you two won't be following her around."

Butler glared at Dick, and grabbed his drink, and made his way toward the pool table.

"You okay?" he asked, looking at Slash.

"I am fine, man. You know me. Fine."

"You look pissed," Butler said.

"Why the fuck are you here?" Slash stopped playing, throwing the pool stick onto the table.

"To be honest, talking to you was easier than having to be near Dick. He may have a woman, but it takes too much of my fucking energy to be with him."

Slash looked over his shoulder.

"I don't want us to fight," Butler said. "We're club brothers. We need to have each other's back. It's how it works."

"I'm not giving up," Slash said. "I want Natalie, and she's going to be mine. I don't give a shit how hard I've got to work. She's mine."

Butler nodded. "I figured as much. Just so you know, I'm not backing down either. Natalie, she's a beautiful woman, but I'm not going to guilt her. We both fight for her, equally." He held his hand out waiting for Slash to shake on it.

Slash didn't shake on it. "I don't shake with a man that I'm about to do battle with."

He smirked.

No matter what, they would be club brothers.

"Okay, place your bets now. Who will win between Slash and Butler? Who will Natalie pick?" Dick said, shouting up, and placing bets. He really was a dick.

Epilogue

One year later

The Skulls came to Piston County for Christmas, and it was a proper full house affair. Simon got to give Tabitha the journal he had handpicked for her, and Chaos Bleeds were able to spend some time without the threat of violence hanging over their heads.

Sinner and Lola stayed true to their word. They waited to get married until Lexie had given birth to little Amelia. Martha also gave birth to a healthy son, Noah. Once Lexie was back to full health, Lola really got to know what it was like to be organized. Lexie brought order to Chaos, and she was in the perfect position of being Devil's old lady.

There was the wedding dress that Natalie drew, and then of course there were caterers, and she asked Angel to cook for them. Of course, Lola got married in a church, and everything just sort of flew by.

Staring out across the ocean, Lola took in the setting sun, and the freshness of the ocean.

Sinner stepped up behind her, wrapping his arms around her slightly swollen stomach.

"What are you thinking, wife?"

She giggled. "I'm thinking that I have never been happier." They were on their honeymoon. Alex from The Skulls owned an island. She didn't even want to think about who he had to kill to get his own island, but she was staring at it. "It's so beautiful."

"Nothing will ever be as beautiful as you."

"You know how to say all the right things."

He pressed a kiss to her neck. "I can't help it. When I'm with you, everything feels so natural."

She closed her eyes and basked in his love.

They had gone through so much together. Their relationship hadn't been an easy thing. Each obstacle they had fought together and apart had led them to this moment. She was pregnant, expecting their first child. She loved him more than anything in the world. Now, she felt like she could give him everything he deserved.

There was nothing holding her back. She was free to love, to grow, and to enjoy a future with him.

Tilting her head to the side, she smiled at him. "Thank you for never giving up on me."

He pressed his lips against hers, and she melted.

"I'll never give up. You're mine, Lola, forever." He held her close, and together they watched the sun set.

Their life was going to be perfect, she just knew it.

The End

www.samcrescent.com

BESTSELLING BBW ROMANCE
SPICY ROMANCE FOR REAL WOMEN

SAM CRESCENT

EVERNIGHT PUBLISHING ®

www.evernightpublishing.com